NO WAY OUT BUT IN

by Belvah Golding

www.xulonpress.com

Write for permission to the address below:

Belvah Golding
182 Horizon Lane
Oceanside, CA 92056
760-630-5207
dalegolding@sbcglobal.net

In appreciation

Without the continual encouragement of my dear husband, Dr. Dale Golding, and our children, Dawn, Susan and Jonathan, this book would never have been written. Warm thanks, too, to my original editor Diane Fillmore of Proclaim Press, who was willing to read the manuscript of a novice and see it through to publication. I must also include our Sunday School class who took the trouble to read it in manuscript form and insist that it had validity. These and many more had a part in this effort. To God by the glory.

Belvah Golding
Whittier, California
October 2002

Forward

Although we know few details of the daily life of Noah's day, the descriptive words and phrases, "corrupt", "wickedness", "filled with violence," "only evil continually," in the sixth chapter of Genesis remind us very much of our own day.. What would it have been like for the women in Noah's family? How could they survive the ridicule and ostracism from all their extended families and friends? Who would be willing to give their daughter to one of Noah's sons when his faith and value system was so different than the rest of the people? How could these women face going into the black, stinking, "tomb" of an ark that had gobbled up all the labor of their hands for their lifetime. These are some of the God-sized problems these women faced with a measure of success.

Half of the people who went into Noah's ark were women, yet the Bible does not give us any of their names. For this reason, in so far as the lives of the women are concerned, this story comes from my own sanctified imagination. We do know, however, from the time line given in the 5th chapter of Genesis, that Noah's father Lamach died just five years before the flood and Methuselah lived right up to the year of the flood. Both of these men could have personally known all the patriarchs. I have endeavored to be scrupulously accurate with any Biblical facts that are given and these form the backdrop for those terrible days.

As we study their struggle to survive, my hope is that it will help us face the increasing darkness of our world today. For us, as for them, there is *"no way out"* of the darkness of this world *"but in"* to the light of God's Kingdom through the Door that is Jesus. When the Door is shut, my prayer is that you will be inside.

Belvah Golding
Whittier, California
October 2000

Prologue

Miriam watched the worn soles of her father's sandals as he climbed ahead of her up the long outside stairway to the roof garden. Each step was slow and deliberate because her father Lomar was helping his grandfather make the climb. She and her brothers followed as closely as they dared, impatiently pushing at each other in an attempt to be first. "Don't push me, Cabal! You'll make me fall," protested Miriam. "Then let me go first. I'm older than you. You should let me go first," Cabal responded crossly. "Children! This is a time to rest and not to quarrel," came Father's voice from above them.

With some muttering seven-year-old Miriam and her two older brothers at last made it to the welcoming coolness of the roof. Father helped Grandfather sit on one of the low benches against the outside wall. Behind them came her mother and baby Leah who was already beginning to walk and talk.

"Here Miriam, watch Leah for a while. She is so quick now. Don't take your eyes off her," Mother instructed.

It was Miriam's favorite time of the day. The work was done and all the family gathered to watch the stars appear and talk of the day's activities.

Her brothers had their pet locusts each tied with a piece of flax fiber and they let them fly around and around their heads with a satisfying buzz. Baby Leah reached her delicate hands for them, laughing with excitement when the boys let them come close. It was a quiet time and the day's troubles seldom intruded at this hour.

"Tell us about when you were young, Grandfather," asked Cabal. "Did you have pet locusts then, too?"

"No. I do not remember having one, but there was a bird once. The world was very different then, but we often sat out under the sky in the evening like this, watching the light fade and the night come. When I was your age Cabal, I still lived in the home of my parents and Grandfather Adam was there to tell us stories. We liked to hear him talk about the garden in the beginning time before there were any thorns."

"Tell us about it Grandfather," Miriam begged. She loved to hear Grandfather talk about the beginning time when everything was new. Of course they had heard it before many times, but Miriam always loved to hear it again.

"Tell us about the animals, Grandfather!" put in Cabal.

"Yes, the animals came first," began Grandfather, "and Adam's first work was to give them all names. What a day that was, getting to know each species and choosing a name that would best suit their personality. But Grandfather Adam said after that long day, that first day, he still felt rather lonely and he didn't really know why."

"But God knew!" put in Miriam.

"Yes, God knew! He knew that Adam had seen all those animals and there were two of every one. But Adam was only one! Of course he was lonely."

"That was when God made Grandmother Eve wasn't it?" piped up Miriam. "I like this part."

"Yes, God caused Adam to go to sleep. His very first sleep after that long busy day of naming all the animals. Then God made Eve from Adam's own rib and when Adam awakened, there she was. Just the right companion for Grandfather. I remember seeing her just once when I was very small.

"He said they used to celebrate that wonderful evening every day. As it would begin to get dark, God Himself would come and walk with them, and they would talk together about that first evening when all God's creation was finished. Then the next day, they rested together, marveling at all that God had made.

"In the evening, about this time, Grandfather Adam and Grandmother Eve would hear His voice calling their names and they would quickly run to Him, their hearts nearly bursting with the joy of His coming. Each day was better than the last as they learned more and more of His thoughts and plans for them.

"Everything was good then. Can you imagine? Everything! No death, no sadness, no fear, no thorns and thistles! Only good! Oh if only..." Grandfather's eyes grew misty and he became silent.

Miriam and the boys began to shift uncomfortably. They knew what was coming and they wanted to hear more of the good times and new discoveries.

"I will never forget hearing him tell of that awful day when they decided to disobey God." His eyes filled with tears.

"'How wise we felt... wiser than God! The serpent made what we were doing so exciting and right. It would be another discovery! How wrong we were!' he would say. If only these young people today could hear him tell it."

"But Grandfather, the Nephilim say we are foolish to obey God. They say that they have been in the heavens and they know much more about Him than anybody. They are very smart and so strong!"

"Do not believe them, Cabal. Grandfather Adam said that the serpent was so beautiful and seemed so wise. But still he was a liar. He did not tell the truth. Don't listen to the Nephilim. The same spirit is in them that was in the serpent.

God said we would all die if we chose to disobey Him and this was true."

"But the Nephilim say that death is just so that the world won't get too full. If nobody died, then where would we put everyone? They say it is just natural to die."

"Does it seem natural to you, Cabal? Is that what you are working for each day...just to die and leave it all behind?" Lomar asked.

"But your father didn't die, did he, Grandfather?" asked Ger, looking up from untangling his locust.

"No, my father did not die. But then he walked with God everyday just like Adam and Eve did in the beginning. He must have heard them tell it hundreds of times just as I did.

""When we heard His voice, it filled our whole bodies with light and joy. Usually in the evening, as night was coming on, He would be there calling us by name and reassuring us about the darkness. He said it was good darkness. He said it was a time for resting and for planning. He told us all that we needed to know to care for the garden. He could have done it all with a word, you know. The garden, I mean. But He wanted our help and our company. He would say, 'This fern likes the shade. Never put it out in the bright sunshine.' Or, 'This tree has grown too large for these roses now. Move them out into the open. They will be happier there.' Oh if only...'"

"Nobody believes that any more, Grandfather," Cabal interrupted, hoping to get Grandfather to move on to a more exciting subject. "They say that the world just grew by itself and Grandfather Enoch just fell in a tar pit or the river."

"Cabal, you do not know what I mean when I say he walked with God. It was not some evening stroll from which he never returned. No! It was that his every daily step was with God whether he was in the house or in the field, not just some times. He talked with God as naturally as he talked with us. He never had needed to go near those unpleasant, smelly tar pits. I was there that day and I saw him sitting quietly in his seat by the door and then he was gone. Just gone! Your father was there too, Lomar. We saw what happened," insisted the frail old man. Cabal just turned away and made a face as if to say, 'What does he know?'

"These young people today are not afraid of disobeying God. They fear all the wrong things. They think nothing of hating and killing each other, or stealing or going from one woman to another. They fear they will miss some pleasure or they fear the Nephilim. But God is the one they should fear. God will judge them! You wait and see. God will not let this wickedness go on forever."

"That's what Uncle Noah keeps saying, but nothing ever happens," said Cabal. "People laugh at him all the time and say he is crazy. He has been building on that ark of wood forever but still nothing has happened."

Miriam's brother often joined in the jeering too, but he didn't admit this at home. If his father asked where he had been, he would say, "Helping Uncle Noah."

Miriam had heard both her brothers laughing and making jokes about Uncle Noah. She wondered how Cabal could lie so easily. She couldn't. God would know. She was sure of that. Grandfather said that God knew everything and she believed him.

"Cabal, the day will come when you will be forced to admit that your Uncle Noah was right. I can only pray that you will be on the right side of the door when it is closed," Grandfather said, fixing his grand nephew with a look so kind that it made Miriam brush back some tears.

"Yes, Grandfather," Cabal said politely but as he turned away, his face twisted in a sneer.

Later that night as Miriam lay in her small sleeping pallet at the foot of her parent's bed, she quietly prayed, "I do believe in you God. I want to walk with you like Grandfather Enoch did. Please God. Show me the way."

Chapter One

As she drew back the curtain to the familiar but now empty room, it was his shoes that she noticed first. They were there, just as he always left them at night, their worn leather straps molded exactly to the shape of his feet. Suddenly all the tears she had not been able to shed came pouring down her face as she knelt and gathered them into her arms. He was gone and she would never see him again! Deep in her heart she felt it was her fault. It was her defense that had brought on that senseless, violent blow that had ended her father's life. How could she go on living, knowing that? Where could she go now to hide?

From long habit she rose and turned back across the open center of the house to the little room where she always found solace in grief. Stepping through the door, she looked at the sleeping platform where her beloved Grandfather had lain so long. Here, too, there was no one. Only an empty room, and the house around her was empty and quiet. Where were her brothers? Her mind raced back, trying to think what she could have done differently.

Suddenly remembering her danger, she ran to her room and gathered the clothing she had come to collect. Her engagement jewels and some dried figs went into her bundle along with two loaves of flat bread and some oranges. Then, glancing hurriedly around she slipped out the back door and through the garden the same way she had fled that awful night. Now, where could she go? She was a danger to any who took her in and any who saw her might tell Koruz where she was. Over and over the events of the past two weeks continued to replay themselves in her mind. She could still hear her brother Cabal's terse whisper, "You'll get us all killed yet with your holier than thou attitude. Just go with him! There isn't any God to care anyway!"

Now hurrying through the gathering darkness she wondered if Cabal had been right. Maybe there wasn't any God after all. Maybe the Nephilim were right. But thinking of them only made her quicken her steps. If only her mind would stop going over and over these past days.

She had been sweeping the garden beside the house that morning when her cousin Laban had approached her. She felt his eyes on her before she looked up. He was standing there greedily watching her every move. At last he spoke.

"I've done it, you know. I've asked my father to arrange our marriage. Now you will have to listen when I talk to you."

A chill settled around her heart as she stooped to get a stubborn leaf from the corner where the walls met. The more she swept at it the tighter it seemed to cling.

I am like that leaf, she thought. *Pressed into a corner with no way to escape. Please God, help me. Pick me up and carry me away. Don't toss me on the garbage heap as I am doing with this leaf.*

Laban started toward her but at that moment her mother's voice from inside the house stopped him.

"Miriam, please hurry. I need you here in the kitchen."

"Yes, Mother, I'm coming," she said, warm relief flooding through her. She kept her eyes on the ground as she passed Laban on the way into the house. His hand reached for her but she was too quick, and she heard him curse as she went through the door.

As she came into the kitchen, her sister giggled and covered her mouth with her hand.

"He asked for you, Miriam. Did he tell you? You'll soon be an old married woman. Aren't you excited?"

"I will not marry him," she said under her breath. "I'd sooner die than marry him."

"I'll marry him then," said her sister, Leah. "I'm sure he'll like me better anyway. You're too fussy. If it were left to you, you'd never get married."

Miriam wondered if that was really true. She worked quickly sorting the yarns to be woven. What would her father say if she refused Laban? No doubt he would be very angry and would insist anyway. Laban's family had good connections in the city and plenty of money. There seemed to be no one who longed to serve God as she did. Only Grandfather and Uncle Noah and his family and they were always too busy and she hadn't seen any of them since the wake for Noah's father five years ago.

As she put away the sorted balls of yarn she heard Grandfather calling from his small bedroom. With a quick step, she moved to his side.

"Yes, Grandfather. Did you call? What can I bring you?"

"Please fetch a little wine, Miriam, I am very thirsty."

Miriam caught up a bowl and went to the goatskin hanging near the door. Carefully she drew a little wine and then filled the bowl with water from the large jar outside the door. She knew just how he liked it and he smiled at her as she handed him the bowl.

"Let me help you sit up, Grandfather. You've been asleep and will be a little stiff I think."

"Thank you, my daughter. You always mix the wine just right and seem to know my needs before I do. Come and sit by me a bit." He took a long drink from the bowl.

"I hear that your marriage is being arranged," he said with a quiet sigh. "I shall greatly miss you in this house."

When Miriam failed to respond, Grandfather lifted his eyes once more to her face, but she quickly turned away so that he would not see the tears that threatened.

"Your father tells me that Laban's family has prospered and that you will have a large house to manage one day. Are you pleased with this, my child?"

Miriam quickly busied herself, straightening the bedding and the pillows around Grandfather. The tears receded and when she could safely speak, she responded, "What bride would not wish for such a future?"

It was a proper answer and Grandfather seemed to accept it. Then he grunted, saying, "What bride indeed! My ears are not very sharp any more, Miriam, but I can hear no joy in your words. I am not so old that I cannot remember the light in my wife's face on our wedding day. It should be a day of joy, not just noise, as it seems to be these days. She was so beautiful! You look a great deal like her, Miriam. Have I told you that before?"

"Yes, Grandfather."

Miriam thought she was safely past the subject of her marriage and into the memories of long ago, but Grandfather was not finished yet.

"Laban comes from the family of my father's brother, I believe. They have not lived in this area for many years. I wonder what brought them here to Uz."

"Laban said it was the Nephilim who offered them the big house if they brought their family business here. I don't know why, but that is what he said."

"What is their business?

"They dye and weave fine linen. There seems to be a very good market for their goods here." She had watched the excitement in her mother and sister when they had bought a new piece of the linen in the market.

"Are they in business with the Nephilim, then?"

"Koruz is a grandson of the Nephilim, and he is the one Laban works for." Miriam's voice was faint and Grandfather glanced at her in an attempt to hear more clearly. She did not meet his eyes. Finally he sighed deeply.

"I ask you again, Miriam; is *this* bride pleased with this marriage?"

The shake of her head was barely discernible.

"Has Laban been cruel to you, my child? Is this why you do not look forward to your marriage?"

"No, Grandfather, he hasn't touched me but his looks turn my heart cold. And he does not love God!" It came out in a rush. "He believes everything that Koruz says and he is already serving them even though he pretends not to be when he is here. Oh Grandfather, what am I to do? Is there no one left who loves God and wants to serve Him? Must I marry one who only thinks of pleasing himself, or them?"

Methuselah stretched out his long bony hand and took her small hand in his.

"Do not be afraid, Miriam. I will speak to your father for you. And we will pray that God in Heaven will give you a husband who is faithful. God knows your desire. We will ask Him for His help."

As Miriam turned to go, she did not see the look of despair that crossed her grandfather's face nor hear him murmur, "Where indeed, Lord? Where indeed?"

Back in the kitchen, the talk turned to the engagement dinner and what the menu should be. Miriam kept her hands busy grinding grain and her head down, hoping no one would ask for her opinion. Engagement dinners were important affairs and all the influential people in the city must be invited. Laban and his family would have to be consulted for their lists. Miriam prayed silently, "Please God, help Father to change his mind."

"You must have all new clothes, Miriam," began her mother. "Perhaps pale green would be the best. We could set it off with a lace border of dark green and make an ivory lining. That color goes well with your light coloring. New sandals too, I think. I saw some beautiful gold-colored ones last week at the market. Perhaps if we hurry, we can go there tomorrow before they are all gone."

"We'd better go today," chimed in Leah. "When people hear that another wedding is coming up, everyone will be looking for their new things."

"Yes, I suppose so. But there is no time today. Tomorrow will have to do."

"If Miriam doesn't kill herself first," chided Leah. "She said she would rather be dead than marry Laban."

Miriam's mother looked quickly at her older daughter.

"Are you not happy with this wedding, Miriam? Surely your father has done well to arrange it and you will have a beautiful home, servants and anything you might want. Does this not please you?" her mother questioned.

"Please Mother, I don't want to seem ungrateful but..." began Miriam.

"Well, I should hope not!" interrupted her mother. "I would hate to think a daughter of mine would be so rebellious as to try to dictate to her parents whom she should marry. It is just not to be considered."

"But he doesn't believe in God, Mother."

"Nonsense! His great, great grandfather was a brother of Enoch. What better religious connections could you want? Anyway, in this day and age, no one pays much attention to those things. It's rather old fashioned to cling to such things now. You must not let your personal feelings for Grandfather spoil this opportunity. It is long past the time for you and your sister to be married."

Miriam could think of no answer to this so she said nothing. When her father and her two older brothers came

20

home for the evening meal, she served them with a quiet face, moving in her efficient way until all were satisfied.

"There was some excitement in the field today," said Cabal, the older of the two boys. "We just finished the harvest in the south field when two very large tigers came strolling across just as if they took that route every day of their lives. They didn't seem to be hungry but some of the boys with dogs chased after them, shouting and throwing stones. It was really strange. The tigers hardly even looked back. They just kept trotting quickly to wherever they were headed."

"Where did they go after they left our field?" Leah asked.

"I don't really know. They were headed north around the west edge of town. I hear there might be good hunting there as quite a lot of game has been seen around there. Maybe they heard it by their tiger grapevine and were on their way to supper."

"Koruz has been looking for a pair like that to put into his 'garden'," said Ger. "Maybe you should get word to him that they have been seen. He might want to send out a hunting party for them. He pays well for such information."

"Laban could take a message for you, Cabal," commented Leah. "He sees Koruz almost every day at work." Leah always seemed to know everything about everybody. Miriam found it hard to imagine just where she picked up all her information.

"Will Laban be coming over tonight, Father?" Cabal asked.

"Most likely he will be bringing his guest list for the engagement dinner."

"I'll talk with him then."

After supper, Miriam helped clear the table and tidy up the kitchen. Then she slipped in to see if Grandfather needed anything and found him soundly sleeping. Taking the tray back to the kitchen, she dealt with the dirty dishes deftly as her mind raced. Somehow she must talk with her father before Laban came this evening, but as she approached the stairs leading to the roof, she heard Laban's voice already in conversation with her father. She was too late.

Instead of joining them, she went on to her bed, wondering what she could do next. She really didn't want to talk with Leah so she lay down and closed her eyes, not really expecting to sleep. But the day had been heavy with emotion and she was tired. It was early morning when she heard Grandfather cough and then call her name quietly.

"Ah, there you are, Miriam," he said as she came in the room. "I have been waiting for you to come. I must have fallen asleep last night and did not get a chance to talk with your father. Perhaps after breakfast you can tell him that I wish to see him."

"Of course, Grandfather," said Miriam, a little surprised that he had remembered. "But I am afraid it is already too late. Laban was here last night with his guest list for the engagement dinner. Mother and Leah have gone to the early market to begin preparations. I don't really think there is anything we can do now."

"Nevertheless, I will try, Miriam. Who knows? Maybe God will answer our prayer in a most unusual manner. Just trust Him."

"I'll try, Grandfather. But my faith is very small."

"Then we will lean our weak faiths against each other, and then they will be twice as strong."

"Surely your faith is not weak, Grandfather."

"Ah Miriam, I have lived many years and seen many disappointments. But I am determined to trust Him even when I can't see any results. I am too old now to change with the times. Still, it has been a very long wait and our enemy likes to whisper that it is all for naught. Sometimes in my dreams he comes and laughs at me for believing. Sometimes I almost believe him. Then I remember my father, his words and his first-hand accounts of his talks with God. How can I doubt such evidence? But the years have been so long."

Miriam went out to prepare the breakfast and deliver Grandfather's message to her father. After breakfast Lomar went to the little bedroom and sat on the low stool beside the sleeping platform. Miriam, sweeping in the back garden, could clearly hear their voices through the open window.

"But I gave my word to Laban, Grandfather. Surely you do not expect me to go back on that, especially now when the guest list is made and the word has begun to spread that there will be an engagement dinner."

"Do events move so swiftly that a guest list that was only delivered last night is already being talked about in the market place?"

"Well, nothing moves faster than the news of a wedding, engagement or a divorce. I'm sure the servants at Laban's home heard the talk and since my wife and younger daughter are already at the market buying who knows what, there can be no doubt of it. Laban has even mentioned it to Koruz and he has already promised to attend."

"I never expected to see the day when Koruz or any of his kind would be dining in this house," Grandfather said with a sigh.

But Miriam's father was not to be discouraged. His eyes brightened with excitement.

"Imagine a man so powerful and smart as Koruz, eating in our humble home. I know how you feel about him. I feel the same, but he is very famous and people fear him almost as though he were a god."

"My son, do not be deceived by his appearance or his strength. He is not a good man. His life is filled with evil continually. Surely we do not need to entertain him here."

"But he is Laban's employer. He told me so last night. There is no way that I can refuse him."

23

"What about your daughter? Surely you care about her wishes. Have you asked her if she is pleased with this marriage?"

"It is because I love her that I have arranged this marriage for her. She will be safe in Laban's house as his wife. You know there are very few safe places for girls these days. But by giving her to Laban, and he is friendly with Koruz, I can perhaps prevent her being taken into the harem of one of the rich merchants in town. You know if they saw her they would want her. Her coloring alone, with her golden hair would make them pay a high price to have her. Better that she is safely married to Laban.

"I know that Laban is not a believer but in these days we can not make that the criterion. We must be practical. It is difficult to keep up with the way things are now.

"Everything is changing so fast. Have you heard that Koruz has developed a plan to bring flowing water into the city so that it will be available to all? Laban says that the plans are drawn and work will begin very soon on that project."

Grandfather sighed and said no more. He had tried. Now he must simply pray.

A week later, on the night of the engagement dinner, Miriam had looked her prettiest in her new gown with the dark, lace-fringed shawl covering her bright hair. The dinner had proceeded as planned. The hired servants had carried dish after dish to the tables of the guests. There seemed to be no end to the variety but finally the fruits were brought in and the serious eating was finished. Miriam had been served at the small family table at the side of the room with her mother and sister and a few of her cousins. None of Noah's family were there.

Koruz and Laban were seated near her father at the head table along with the more important visitors of the city. Miriam had felt she was living through a nightmare as she endured the bold glances of the men. Leah laughed and chattered happily with her cousins and Miriam's mother kept a strong eye on the servants to see that the important guests were being properly served. Musicians had been hired and were tuning their instruments impatiently, waiting for the signal from Miriam's father. At last he stood and tapped the table for silence.

Miriam's heart felt like stone as she listened to her father's voice, warm and jovial, making their guests welcome and preparing them for his special announcement. At last she heard him call her by name and ask her to come and stand between he and Laban.

"Oh, God, where are you? Are you truly the living God? Help me, God. Save me from this marriage," Miriam cried silently. With head lowered, she took her place between Laban and her father. The golden purse was passed between the two men and Miriam's father gently placed his great work-worn hand on her shoulder. Miriam straightened a bit under the pressure of his encouragement but as she did so, the shawl covering her head slipped back and her crowning-glory was revealed. Quickly she pulled the shawl back in place but not before gasps of surprise had escaped the lips of those seated nearest them.

Before her father could continue, Koruz rose and with his powerful eyes on her, said to Laban, "What have you been keeping from me here. You did not tell me your wife-to-be was such a rare beauty. Before we finish this party, let me talk with this young woman's father.

"Lomar, whatever Laban has arranged with you, I will double it if you will give this young woman to me."

Laban's face drained of all color. He tried to speak but a look from Koruz silenced him. Koruz was not only rich, but big as well, easily head and shoulders taller than any man in the room. Never had he thought that Koruz would do such an unthinkable thing as this. The outrage of it choked him.

Miriam stood frozen for a moment and then hearing her father's low voice say, "Go Miriam," she had fled back through the kitchen and out into the back garden. She could hear her father's voice as she leaned weakly against the back of the house.

"Now, Koruz, you are my guest and I would like to honor your request, but Laban and I already have an agreement. My daughter has been given to him. She is not available to be bargained for as you would like to do." Almost he added, "Like an animal!" but innate courtesy held back these rude words. Instead he continued, "Please, let us eat and drink to their health. Musicians, give us some music!"

Koruz, glancing around and sensing the disapproval in the atmosphere had inclined his head slightly to show his deferral to the older man, but in his eyes there was no retreat; the message there was clear. He had seen Miriam and he wanted her for himself.

For Miriam the rest of the evening passed in a fog of fear and confusion.

Chapter Two

"Wasn't he exciting?" bubbled Leah as the family were putting the house in order after all the visitors had gone.

"Did you ever see such a handsome man? I wish my hair was blond like yours. Then maybe he would look at me."

"Leah, such talk is not acceptable in this house," scolded her father.

"She is just over-wrought by the party and food," her mother interposed. "Leah, go to bed before you make yourself sick with all this excitement. We can talk about it in the morning."

Miriam lingered near her father as the rest of the family and servants made their ways to bed. She looked at him with large frightened eyes.

"No Miriam, I will not let him have you," he said to her unspoken question.

"This is why I have been planning your marriage to Laban, just to prevent such a thing. Don't be afraid. I will not let Koruz have you."

"Thank you Father. I see now that you are planning for my good," Miriam whispered faintly.

Later as she lay on her bed, she cried out to God in despair.

"I am in your hands. There is no place here where I can be safe. If I refuse Laban, Koruz will have me. Surely Koruz will not go so far against our customs as to take me from another man's house, especially when they are friends."

Yet deep in her heart she knew that Koruz was capable of that or anything. He seemed to have no conscience or fear of anything at all. His cold smooth face looked evil to her. There were no human feelings in the eyes, no warmth or light.

"God, I come to you and ask you to keep me safe even in the house of Laban," she prayed as she lay in a ball around her knotted stomach.

Laban was an early visitor the next day. He asked to speak to Miriam's father alone. Miriam, working quietly in the back garden could not keep from hearing the voices from her father's quarters. Miriam's father was warm in his greetings.

"You are early this morning, Laban. This newly engaged man cannot wait to see his intended, I think. Well the days will pass quickly and soon she will be yours."

Laban accepted Lomar's offer of a chair.

"Miriam, bring us some warm water and fresh oranges," Lomar called, clearing a place on his table to receive them.

Miriam hurried to the pot that was kept boiling in the morning and drew the water, adding a few mint leaves to each cup. Oranges were abundant and she loaded the tray with a bright bowl full. Laban did not look at her as she entered the room. She quietly placed the tray on the table and poured the boiling water on the leaves. Then with a respectful bow, she went back to her task outside.

Laban took his cup in his hands, turning it around and around. Finally, he looked at Lomar briefly. Lomar was busy with his own drink and did not see the terror that was revealed in the look. At last Laban sighed and began.

"I wish to thank you for the beautiful dinner with which you honored us last night. It was truly memorable and I humbly thank you and acknowledge my debt to you." He paused, moistening his lips from the cup before continuing.

"I had a visit from Koruz this morning. I had not even finished my breakfast." He was not quite able to keep the tremor out of his voice.

"His business must have been urgent to bring him out early after such a late night."

"He was very blunt. He did not take time for greetings or a warm drink. He just told me flatly that I am not to marry Miriam."

Lomar grew very quiet in his chair, as though he were gathering himself into some hidden place deep within. Finally he said in a tightly controlled voice, "He has no right to make such a demand. The engagement has been announced and I see no reason to change that now. You must simply stand up to him, Laban. Don't let his great size intimidate you."

Laban stood nervously and began to pace.

"It is not that simple, I'm afraid. If I displease him, I will have no business, no home, and no money to offer Miriam."

"But you can take your business elsewhere, can't you? Not that I want to see Miriam move far away, but if that is the only way, then I will not object."

Laban sat down near his future father-in-law. He was sweating and his face was pale and stiff.

"It's more than the business, Uncle," Laban whispered hoarsely. "He promised that he would kill me if I proceed with the marriage plans." He paused and licked his lips nervously. "I believe him, Uncle. He would not hesitate."

There was silence for several minutes.

"But surely he would not really do such a thing, Laban. It is wrong. God will hold him responsible for that. He can not just do as he pleases."

"He does not fear God at all, and he makes his own rules. I didn't believe all those stories I had heard about him before, but now he has told me plainly with his own lips what he will do if I stand in his way. He said he had been searching for just such a bride to add to his collection.

"It's not the first time he has done this. I had heard stories about it but I really thought it didn't matter. So he wanted many women. Many men have such thoughts. No one takes much notice of it these days. It is like having a lot of cattle, or many sheep."

The older man's face darkened with anger.

"But Laban, my daughter is not some sheep to be bartered away to the highest bidder. She has been a faithful daughter to me. She has cared for my grandfather kindly and humbly. She is a precious treasure to me. Do you think that I will give her to Koruz, knowing what he is like?"

"I don't think you have any choice, Uncle."

"But surely...!"

"What you do about this is your own affair, Uncle. But I must withdraw my request for Miriam's hand."

"We will talk about this again. Perhaps Grandfather will have some suggestion. I will talk with him about it first. Don't despair, Laban."

But Laban turned toward the door, not even looking at his uncle as he said, "I won't be back. I don't dare. You can send the dowry to me later. I am sorry I have brought trouble to your house. But if you give Miriam to Koruz, you will not have further problems, I'm sure."

"But what about Miriam? Don't you care at all what happens to her?"

Laban did not pause or look up as he moved out the door. A mumbled "Sorry" was all that reached the listening ears of both Miriam and her father.

Miriam, outside the window, stood frozen with terror. She did not hear the weary sigh that escaped her father's lips. He sat for a long time, wondering what he could do next. Then heavily, he arose and moved toward the little room where his grandfather lay. He would talk to Methuselah. Perhaps he would have an answer to this problem.

Grandfather was awake when he entered and the two men looked at each other in silence for some minutes.

"I have been wrong, Grandfather," Lomar said with a sigh. "Wrong to think that we could co-exist with such a man as Koruz. Laban was just here and has withdrawn his request for Miriam. He says I must give her to Koruz instead. Koruz!" He spat the word in anger. "Can you see this house joined to the house of Koruz? Yet, I do not wish to anger him either. We must continue to live in the same city. We must find some way out of this. What can we do that will spare Miriam and yet not endanger our own household?"

Methuselah lay quietly, thinking. The pain that he felt eased itself with silent tears that coursed down his deeply lined cheeks. At last he said, "Perhaps we could send her to a distant relative. One of my sons lives in the coastal city of Tyre. Perhaps he has a son she could marry."

"That would only bring the wrath of Koruz down on all of us. If only she were a plain girl, this would not have happened. I should not have brought her to the table during the party, but it is our custom to do so. How could I have known?"

"I know nothing else to do but to pray that the God of Heaven will have mercy on this girl and on us," Methuselah said quietly.

"Yes, pray, by all means, but I'm afraid even God cannot help us now."

Events had moved so swiftly then that they seemed a blur. The awful day when Koruz came back demanding her... her father's stout refusal... Koruz offering more money... her father pleading for more time to make arrangements.

Koruz had gone then, saying he would be back the next day. Mealtime was strained and silent that night but Miriam could not escape the dark looks from her brothers and the closed-up face of her mother. They were blaming her for this problem, she knew. But her father was determined even though Miriam heard her mother arguing with him late into the night.

"Just give him the girl," her mother had said. "You really have no choice about it. You know that Koruz gets what he wants in the end. You only endanger the rest of us by your refusal."

"No, Adah, I have made many wrong choices in my life, but I can not do this thing. Think of Miriam. What kind of life would she have? Has she not been a faithful daughter all these years?"

"Yes, too many years! She should have married long ago. I've told you that many times."

"But Grandfather loves her and she is good with him. I thought he would be gone long ago, but still he needs her. If Laban will not have her, let her stay here and take care of Grandfather."

"Koruz will have something to say about that! He will not leave us in peace now. You know that."

"But don't you see that I must at least try to do what is right?"

"What is right about putting the whole family in jeopardy? And he has offered a great deal of money. We could easily hire someone to care for Grandfather with that money."

As Miriam lay listening to this argument that seemed to go on forever, she wondered if it wouldn't be simplest and best just to go with Koruz. That way the family would be safe. *I will just sacrifice myself for them*, she thought, but in her heart there came no echo of peace or joy at doing what was right.

"God, help me. I don't know what is right any more. Everything seems wrong. I wish I could walk with you and talk with you like Grandfather Enoch did. But that was a long time ago. Nobody walks with You now. Maybe not even Uncle

Noah because he is too busy with his boat. Oh, God, if you can hear me, tell me what to do."

Swiftly, as if in answer, into her mind came the gentle face of Grandfather.

"Oh, yes. Why didn't I think of it before? I can ask Grandfather what to do." And with that thought sleep came at last.

The next morning, she was up early to take warm water to Grandfather and help him get ready for the day. He was awake as usual when she stepped quietly into the little room.

"I've brought you some warm water, both for drinking and to wash with, Grandfather. Did you sleep well?"

"I'm not sure, Miriam. Perhaps for a while. I spent much of the night praying about the problems that have come up with Koruz."

"I hope God has told you what we should do. Then maybe you can help me know what is right." Miriam moved about the bed straightening it.

"Mother and my brothers think I should just go quietly to Koruz in order to save the family trouble. I am willing to do that if it is best. But I don't feel any peace inside when I think of it. I don't know what is right or wrong any more. I don't want my family to suffer because of me. But I don't want to disobey God either. Would I be sinning to go to Koruz? Or would I be sinning if I didn't go? It's so confusing!"

"My child, that sounds very noble and good to sacrifice your own pleasure for the family. But you have forgotten that your father has said 'no'. He is responsible for this decision, not you. Leave it in his hands. Don't do a thing just because it seems noble unless you know in your heart that it is the right thing to do."

Miriam helped Grandfather sit up and straightened his bedding, finding comfort in the familiar daily tasks. But her mind still wrestled with the conflicting wrongs confronting her. She had brought in Grandfather's breakfast and was sweeping the room before either of them spoke again. They often enjoyed these long companionable silences between them, each busy with his own thoughts. It was Grandfather who broke the silence.

"I know your dilemma, Miriam. Both ways seem wrong. This may mean that there is another way that we have not thought of yet. I am asking God to show us His way. There is always a right thing to do."

"Always? If there is, I don't know what it could be," Miriam said with a half-sob trembling beneath the surface of her words.

"His ways are higher than our ways. He will show you, Miriam. When the time comes, you will know what to do. When we truly want to do right, God always is there to lead the way."

As these words came back to her now, this promise seemed very hollow. Koruz had come later that day. He had demanded that she go with him at once. Her father had been conciliatory, respectful and yet firm in his refusal.

"Miriam is very precious to me. She cares for my grandfather who is of a great age. Perhaps when he is gone, we can talk again about this, but I can not give her to you now."

Koruz was not accustomed to being refused by anyone. From his earliest days, he had always gotten just what he wanted, both because of his powerful father and later because of his great size and wealth. Now he towered over Lomar. Miriam, watching from behind the lattice wall, saw the awful blow start—a deliberate straightening and stiffening of the hand, the long arcing swing of his arm. Unable to bear it Miriam had hidden her face in her hands.

Before the blow connected, Miriam heard her father's desperate cry, "Miriam, run!"

The sickening sound of the blow drew her eyes in spite of herself. She watched in horror as her father crumpled to the floor, his neck obviously broken. Then she had turned and ran. Out the back door, down through the olive trees, into the denser foliage of the orange grove. Behind her she heard the voice of Koruz, shouting, "Find her and bring her to me," and the sandaled feet of several men, running after her through the grove.

At first she ran blindly, seeing only the form of her father on the floor. Then she realized where she must go. Through the heavy leaves she could see the back wall of her father's property. As a child she and her brothers had known of the opening under the wall where some animal had dug a way in long ago. Now she moved toward this, desperate to reach it before she could be seen. The wall was overhung with branches of smaller shrubs from which they gathered seasoning leaves. Plunging into this thicket, she was almost to the wall, when a great flurry of noise and leaves erupted in front of her. She almost fainted with fright as she found herself looking into the face of a very large, startled tiger. With one bound it sailed over her into the orange grove.

She stood paralyzed for a long moment and then hearing again, in her mind, her father's command, "Miriam, run!" she flung herself into the narrow opening and out under the wall. Once on the other side, she could quickly lose herself from sight among the standing shocks of wheat, which had been left there to dry.

As she ran, the noise behind her over the wall turned to shouts of terror. Her pursuers must have met the tiger as unexpectedly as she had and were thrown into confusion.

It was yet daylight, so she ran quickly around a large shock of grain in the middle of the field, plunged into it, and drawing her body into a ball, carefully re-arranged the sheaves over the opening. In the semi-darkness, she could see nothing but the face of her father, neck twisted at an odd angle, eyes staring but seeing nothing. She could still, in the distance, hear the shouts and curses. Once she heard the great voice of Koruz demanding that his men "forget the tiger, and find the girl." But apparently the tiger was not so easily forgotten, especially when it was confronted with so many men and so much noise.

"Open the gate, so it has a way out," one voice shouted.

"No, don't let it get away. We will capture it later. I want its coat."

"Look out! It is heading for the wall."

There was a great screaming bellow and then silence. Muted voices reached her, giving commands and making plans. She could no longer understand the words. Once she thought she heard her mother scream but it was cut short abruptly and she heard no more at all until darkness fell.

Through the night, Miriam fell into a light doze, only to be jerked awake by the stunning thought.

My father is dead! Dead! What can I do now? He told me to run so I ran. Now he is dead. What about Grandfather? Who will care for him? Is he still alive or did they kill him too? Maybe my father is not dead. Maybe he needs my care. Surely I could hear the mourners if he were dead. She peered out into the darkness and decided it was near morning. Stretching her cramped legs, she wiggled out of the shock and stood uncertainly, wondering what she should do. *I must find out what has happened.*

Picking her way carefully across the field in the darkness she soon found herself at the hole under the wall. She crept through it, wondering if the tiger was still inside the garden. As she pushed aside the bushes she was drenched with the heavy dew that had gathered on the leaves. The cold and wet added to the trembling that she seemed unable to control. Nothing moved as she passed the orange grove and moved under the olive trees to the back of the house. All was dark and quiet. Where were the mourners? There should be lights and many people about, sitting with the body until the burial.

Hardly breathing, she drew open the back door and slipped toward Grandfather's room. It was still so dark that she had to feel her way across the mat to the bedside. Bending down, she was relieved to hear quiet breathing.

"Grandfather," she whispered. "It's Miriam. Are you awake?"

"Oh, Miriam! I was just praying that God would bring you to me. Are you all right? Has God delivered you out of their hand until now?"

Miriam found the tears rolling down her cheeks.

"Yes, Grandfather, I hid in the field. But what about Father? I was so sure he was dead. But there are no mourners. What happened?"

"My child," Methuselah whispered with a sob shuddering through his bony, withered body, "it is an evil day that I have lived to see. Not even proper respect for the dead. Yes my child, your father is dead. But Koruz ordered his men to take him and bury him secretly and warned your brothers not to say anything to anyone. Imagine! I'm not quite sure what happened. Something about a tiger, and Koruz being injured. Then they simply took your mother and sister and left."

"My mother and sister? Why?"

"I'm not sure, Miriam. Perhaps to prevent them talking. They said something—that maybe there were more blond children in the lineage. Oh Miriam, it is an evil day."

"It's all my fault, Grandfather. I'm a murderer! Oh what can I do now?" Her voice rose as the awfulness of the night took possession of her mind.

Grandfather stifled her next words with his bony hand.

"Miriam! You must keep very quiet! There is still great danger but whatever happens, remember; Koruz is the murderer! Never forget that! Not you! And your father died an honorable death in defending you. You must honor him for that.

"But I must warn you that you cannot stay here. Your brothers have vowed to find you and bring you to Koruz. You must go quickly now. Go to the house of Noah. He will shelter you."

"But what about you, Grandfather. Who will care for you?"

"I am old, Miriam. Perhaps my time has come. But you must go quickly now before your brothers wake and find you here. Go! And God go with you!"

Hearing a stir from her brother's bedroom, Miriam let herself quickly out the back door and retraced her steps through the garden. Where could she go? Shivering with wet and cold, her fear was so strong that it drove out all other thoughts as she made her way back toward the grain field.

Now as she looked back at that terrible night, it seemed a lifetime ago. Could it really have been only one week that she had spent hiding by day and searching for food by night? Today she had risk approaching the house during the day only to find it empty and even Grandfather gone too.

All week she had struggled with his advice. Had it been a command? "Go to Noah. He will hide you."

But her grief and feeling of guilt for her father's death would not let her even start toward Noah's place. It was far on the northern outskirts of the city. It would take a whole day to walk there and she dare not go by day. Could she find her way at night? There seemed no other course.

Sitting with her back to the wall beneath the heavy foliage that had been her refuge most of the week she made a meal of oranges and figs. Then when it was truly dark, she began to move silently down the dark streets carrying her small bundle of clothing and food. Here and there a dog came out to bark and occasionally she met others hurrying toward home but she kept her head down and no one spoke to her.

As she neared the center of the city, she realized that she did not know which of the narrow darkened streets led out to the north side. There were so many lanes and streets. How could she know which one to take?

As she stood uncertainly, Grandfather's words again came back to her. "If you truly want to do what is right, God will lead you."

"If only I could believe that, maybe this knot in my stomach would go away. Please God, show me the way. I really do want to do what is right, I think. I just don't know what right is any more."

From her right came the sound of men walking hurriedly in her direction. She drew back further into the shadow and waited. Three men came into view and Miriam's heart nearly stopped as she realized the tallest of them was Koruz himself. His face was bandaged and he carried his arm in a sling. His fierce eyes seemed to pierce the very darkness and she drew her shawl over her face, giving silent thanks for the dark brown fabric.

"She can't simply have disappeared. Someone surely has seen her. She has to eat. She must sleep somewhere. You just have not talked to enough people or offered enough money," Koruz was saying.

"We'll find her. It's just a matter of time. Her brothers say that she has not been home but I have put a watch on that place just to be sure."

"Did you station a guard at the back as well as the front? Remember she found a way out of the garden or we would have had her last week."

"The back is open fields and a watcher would have no place to conceal himself. But they patrol around constantly. They would see her if she were there."

"Fool! She has probably slipped in and out under your very nose."

Koruz started to lift his arm as though he would strike the other, but movement brought a grimace of pain and a curse instead of a blow. As they hurried on down the street, talking, Miriam drew a long shaky breath and began to make her way down the lane in the opposite direction. Now she knew that she must not let any one see her. Even at Noah's home there would be servants and workers coming and going. Still she pushed on, wanting to put as much distance between herself and Koruz as she could before morning.

The dark lanes at last gave way to gardens and more scattered houses. Now there were fewer places to hide and she hurried along, looking for some place where she would be safe when daylight came. Her clothing was wet now from the mist that watered the earth every night and she shivered miserably.

"Oh God, please guide me," she moaned. "Show me where to go. I have never been this far from home alone before. Lead me to some place safe."

She had been walking for hours now and her legs were so tired that she thought she must sit down and rest a little while. But suddenly from the field at her right came a noisy commotion. Something big was moving toward her. Some animal made chuffing sounds as it pushed its way through the bushes at the edge of the field.

Miriam began to run then, in spite of her tiredness. There seemed to be a beaten path just there and she realized that she could see it dimly. Somehow, the darkness was not as dark as it had been. Morning was coming! She must find a place to hide.

She had followed the little path for what seemed like a mile or more when directly in front of her stood perhaps the ugliest beast she could imagine. Even in the dim gray of that predawn hour she could see that it stood more than half as tall as she and had a long hog-like snout from which protruded two great curved tusks. At the sight of Miriam, it snorted but stood its ground.

Miriam skidded into a new direction and ran all the faster when a glance over her shoulder told her the beast was following her. Ahead there seemed to be great piles of things, maybe stacks of straw, she couldn't see well enough to tell. Then suddenly the path ended at a wooden ramp. It was leaning against a great dark building that seemed to tower over her to the sky. It was so black that it seemed to give off darkness. In the dim light, Miriam could see what appeared to be a deeper darkness at the top of the ramp. It might be an open door. She was just about to turn and make her way around this building when the beast that had been following her came charging through the grass, directly at her. This was too much to bear. Up the ramp she fled, hoping the creature would not follow her. At the top she looked back, but there was the beast, beginning to climb the ramp toward her.

She plunged into the darkness, down a long passageway, fumbling and bumping things in the darkness. Then her hand touched a round, somewhat smooth, pole. Feeling hurriedly she realized that she had come to a ladder. The sound of the animal's hard little hooves was still coming toward her in the darkness. Up the ladder she scrambled until she could find no more handholds. She had climbed a great way and now she carefully stepped onto what seemed to be a solid floor. Wanting more distance from the edge, she stepped forward only to find herself falling through the darkness.

"Oh God!" was all the prayer she had time for before she found herself tumbling into a great pile of sweet smelling hay. She gratefully pulled her wet, trembling body as deeply into the hay as she could, then held her breath to see if she was still being followed.

For long minutes she waited, not daring to breathe. Only silence. Then in the distance she heard a pig-like grunt and heard hard little hooves retreating until she could no longer hear anything. Slowly she drew a long shaky breath.

"I wonder where I am," she thought. "I am so cold. But at least I am out of sight. Maybe I'll be safe here for a little while so I can rest."

Waves of weariness from the long night of walking washed over her. She closed her eyes and felt as though she were spinning down into impenetrable depths. In spite of the wetness of her clothes and the coldness that seemed to penetrate to her inmost being, she slept. She slept and dreamed that she was safe in her own bed and that a warm blanket had just been laid over her. In her dream, she could feel the comforting brush of her father's whiskers as he bent over her to bid her God's blessing for the night. Slowly she grew warm. The shivering stopped and deep dreamless sleep claimed her.

Chapter Three

Noah stood in the early morning light, looking at the long black creation that towered over the surrounding fields. It had been so long in the building. One hundred years! Now it was finished. Yesterday he and his sons had put the last coat of pitch on the outside. The inside was already done. The smell was strong and the morning breeze seemed to be holding its breath to avoid it.

"Dear Lord God, I hope I got it right," he murmured. I'm not really a boat builder. I'm a keeper of animals. I know the soil and the plants and what foods will keep my family healthy. I learned to lay stone, but never how to build a boat and especially one so large."

For Noah, oldest brother of Lomar, praying was a natural as breathing. His daily life was always open before God and he discussed every problem with Him, often aloud. His town mates laughed at him, saying he was mad, or just talking to himself but he could no more change this life long habit than he could stop breathing. Nor did he want to.

"If you hadn't told me how, each step of the way," he continued, "I could never have finished this enormous raft. But will it float, Lord? It is so heavy, all those huge beams and braces, all those endless barrels of pitch. Will the food that we have stored be enough? How can I know? You never told me how long we would be in there. Show me what else is needed. I need your guidance today, Lord."

Near the great dark door in the side of the ark, he could see Japheth, his eldest son, watching a pair of deer that were delicately moving toward that opening. Noah smiled.

"Thank you for my boys, Lord. They were so long in coming; I thought you had forgotten me. But now I have three strong sons. Thank you for these boys. Thank you for their wives. Only Japheth, Lord, he still needs a wife. Where will I find a good girl for him: one that is pure and who will be faithful to him? Wherever she is, Lord protect her. Keep her safe. Don't let the Nephilim touch her. You know how they are, Lord. Protect my wife and my sons' wives too."

As he spoke, he turned and looked at the solid stone house that had been his home now for centuries. The little window on the end caught his eye. It opened into the small room where his own father had spent his last days. He had died only five years ago.

"And what about my grandfather, Lord? When they brought him to me two days ago, he was so weak he couldn't even tell me why Lomar had sent him to me. And the servants who brought him were so strangely silent. They seemed afraid. Be merciful to Grandfather. Let him depart in peace when it is Your time. He has outlived all his sons. He is my only living link who remembers Adam now. Be merciful to him and to me, Lord."

Noah sat on the stone seat that was under the lattice sheltering the front gate and buried his face in his hands. He thought of the day before him and the rising anger of the people of the town. They were growing more and more hostile.

"Unless You protect us, the people will kill us all. You know their hearts, Lord. They think only of evil all the time. They have grown so violent. It's painful to see. Do you feel this pain too? Even my own relatives, except for Lomar, have forgotten you. He still seems to try to follow you but his sons mock me with the rest. They don't fear you any more. It's not popular to believe in you Lord. It's not modern! They won't believe me. I've told them so many times that You will judge the world, if they don't repent. I've pleaded with them to join me in the lifeboat, but they just laugh, laugh and throw stones and make obscene jokes. Must they all die, Lord? Can you not turn their hearts back to You?"

Noah felt a light touch on his sleeve and opening his eyes, he found a small monkey peering up into his face. The vertical lines between its eyes reminded him somehow of his dear, long-suffering wife, Evalith. He reached his pitch-stained hand to the monkey and closed his eyes once more. The monkey busily began grooming the pitch from his fingers.

"Help my wife, Lord. She gets so worried. She works so hard and all her "friends" tell her to leave me. They laugh at her too for being a faithful wife to me. She hardly ever goes out now because of them. Thank you for her, Lord. I don't know what I would do without her. But it's hard for her. Please help her."

A gentle nudge against his leg drew Noah's attention away from his morning prayers. Looking down, he smiled into the face of his big golden and black friend. The tiger had come to the ark only a week ago and had spent many nights inside. Noah reached down and patted the handsome head with his work-worn hand. A little scratch behind the ear brought a satisfied twisting of the head clearly signaling a desire for more of the same. The monkey quickly retreated to the lattice above.

"No more this morning, my fine friend. I must get to work. And you must stay out of sight or someone will make a coat out of your beautiful fur. Go on now, back inside. I don't want to lose you. You have more sense than my human friends, don't you?"

The tiger turned back toward the path that led to the ark and Noah stood and walked to the edge of the wide field. It was white now, ready for harvest. He pulled a head of grain and husked it between his palms. The kernels were plump and as he tasted them, they were sweet and ripe. They must not waste a day. The harvest must begin today.

In the kitchen, Evalith, his wife, was bringing the corn cakes from the hearth. The milk jug stood ready on the table and his daughters-in-law were busy cutting fruit and cheese.

"Good morning, Noah. Did you find everything as it should be at the ark this morning?" Evalith greeted.

"Yes, God has kept it safe through the night. I can hardly believe it is really finished. How is Grandfather this morning? Could he speak to you at all?"

"No, not yet. He seemed to know me and tried to ask me something but I couldn't tell what he said," Evalith answered. "But he was able to drink a bit of warm milk and then slept again."

"Did you see the tigers this morning, Father?" This from Japheth who had just come in and who loved animals more than people, it seemed.

"Yes, the male came out and begged for a bit of an ear scratch. I hope they will stay out of sight. Koruz would love to catch them, and you know what that would mean."

"The women at the well were talking about Koruz this morning," said Deborah, the tall, stately wife of Shem, the second of the brothers. "It seems he has been hurt somehow. There is even a rumor that the tiger attacked him. I don't know what is the truth of the story," Her hair, hidden under her head cloth, was long and dark. Her eyes held a hint of laughter in their dark brown depths. To her husband, she was the most beautiful of all women.

"Cor told me that he has a long deep gash in his face and another in his arm," added Loma, whose darkly tanned face was fringed with errant black curls that just would not be completely contained under her head cloth. She giggled as she added, "The girls were saying that maybe it will leave a scar that will spoil his good looks."

"I wonder if the tiger bit is true," mused Japheth. "And if it is, whether it is our tiger or some other. They are not common in this area. Maybe we should shut our tigers in the ark for safekeeping. What do you think, Father?"

"No, God has told me nothing about closing the doors. They must be open for all who wish to enter."

"But what if Koruz comes looking for them and corners them in the ark?" asked Ham as he helped himself to the corn cakes, smearing them with fig jam. Ham's tall frame took a lot to fill it up.

"We will have to leave that problem to the Lord. He knows all about it and we will just have to trust His guidance on this.

"Today we must get to work on that field. It is fully ready this morning and we need to get the grain stored in the ark as soon as possible." As he spoke, Noah finished the last of his grapes and pushed back from the long wooden table. The boys grabbed hands full of the big green grapes from the bowl and followed their father out the door.

"Girls," Evalith began briskly, "we must pick the rest of the grapes today and get them put on the racks to dry. Take those that are already dry into the storage shed so the boys can carry them to the ark this evening." As she spoke, Evalith began clearing the table. She was a short comfortable woman with a cheerful face marred only by the worry lines that had grown deep between her eyes. She was not young but like her husband, she was not old either. Mature. That best described her.

When she had finished her kitchen work, she went once again to the bedroom where her husband's grandfather lay. He was very still but when she spoke his name, Methuselah opened his eyes. He seemed to be expecting someone, and his eyes left hers immediately to look behind her toward the door. Then with a sigh he tried to speak. Evalith could not make it out. She changed his bedding, swept and tidied the room, offered Grandfather a bit more water which he swallowed with difficulty and then carried the bedding out to be washed. Long years of tending Noah's own father made these chores almost automatic.

In the fields the three men worked methodically, cutting the grain with the tools that were made by Tubal-Cain and his sons. Noah had made the long trip east to the city called Enosh when he had heard about their forge. Tubal-Cain had found a way of working with both iron and bronze and now he supplied the whole region with these sharp cutting tools. As Noah watched the boys work, his thoughts turned to God.

"What a blessing these tools are, Lord, and the axes that I used in the cutting of the trees for the ark. Surely you must have shown Tubal-Cain this secret, just as you showed me how to build the ark. When I was a child, we did not have such things. But then, just when I needed them, they were there. Truly the secret things belong to You but those that are revealed are for us and for our children. How sad it is that men have turned these good gifts into weapons for harming each other. Oh God, we are truly a wicked race!"

Noah turned and made his way toward the ark that stood out blackly against the white fields. He must prepare the area for the spreading of the newly cut grain. He felt such urgency to get it into the ark that he would not wait for it to dry in the field. On the upper deck, with the free flow of air, it would dry soon enough. Then they would thresh it there and store the grain in the bins he had built. He was just starting up the ramp when a disturbance at the far edge of the field made him turn. Through the field of ripe grain, some animals were moving. He could only see their broad hairy backs, dark against the surrounding grain. He waited until one lifted its head and he could see it was a bear with its mate following not far behind.

"Come in, my good friends. Come in. I have been waiting for you. But look at the trail you have made through the field! That will give the boys a bit of extra work, eh. Come then. I have a place made just for you two."

Noah turned and moved on up the ramp looking back at the two bears. They snuffled a bit with their heads swaying from side to side but they followed him obediently as he moved down along the dark corridor and down another ramp to a snug corner on the lower deck. The bears seemed to know it was meant for them and they moved in unhesitatingly and lay down on the straw that had been spread there months ago. They wrinkled their noses and sneezed at the strong odor of pitch, but they did not leave.

Noah strode back up the ramp and climbed the ladder to the third deck. This was where the grain could dry. His intelligent blue eyes missed nothing as he studied the board floor for tightness. Yes, it would hold the smallest kernel and be easily swept after threshing. Japheth had cleaned it well yesterday, just as he had told him. He was a good boy, his Japheth.

Evalith sat beside the worn table and nimbly plucked the grapes from the stems packing them into cakes and wrapping them in clean linen clothes. Her mind was struggling with the sense of hurry that Noah seemed to be feeling these days. But what about Japheth? How could they move into the ark without a wife for Japheth? Where could they find a girl for him? It was a pity about Rhoda. She would have made him a good wife. She blamed herself for what had happened. She should have insisted on an early marriage. Noah would have brought her into this home to keep her safe. But how could she know what would happen, and in broad daylight too! When the rioting gang of boys had finished with her, her poor body was lifeless and her features marred almost beyond recognition. "Forgive us Lord, for not protecting her, for not praying more carefully for her. I thought she was safe in the house of her father. I thought her brothers would defend her. Oh God, it is a heavy weight on my soul, how much more on Japheth. It's been two years Lord, but still my heart grieves. And still you have not shown us a wife for Japheth. Please God."

Evalith paused for some moments thinking. "I know. I know. Noah always says You are never late. You always start in time. I just wish I could feel as calm about all this as he does. He never seems to worry. I wish I were like that. And now Grandfather is here. How could we ever care for him in the ark?"

Deborah coming in just then caught only her last words. "Care for who, Mother?"

"Oh, I was just asking God how we could ever care for Grandfather in the ark. Noah keeps talking as though we must move in very soon and I was just counting up my worries I guess. And what about Japheth? He really must have a wife."

"I know, Mother. We were so sure when we found Rhoda that God had provided and then when she was killed it seemed like either we were all wrong or maybe God couldn't protect her. I don't really understand that."

"I had thought maybe Miriam, you know, the daughter of Lomar, would be the one and then the boys heard that she was to be betrothed. Nothing seems to make any sense anymore," sighed Evalith. "Shem says that none of the families will even consider giving their daughter to Japheth. They think because Loma and I have no children that there must be something wrong or we are under some curse or something. And what can we say to that. We *don't* have any children and look how long Shem and I have been married. Do you think we are under a curse, Mother? Noah doesn't seem worried about it. Maybe we should be more trusting, but as the months stretch into years we can't help but wonder."

Evalith shook her head as if to clear away the questions. "Here take these rounds to the shed. There is too much to do to waste time worrying."

As Noah turned and moved toward the door he stopped and a smile spread across his face. Walking toward Noah from the direction of the ramp came two wart hogs. Their hard hooves beat a tattoo on the cypress boards as they moved past Noah and clattered down the ramp to the lower deck.

"What incredibly ugly faces these have, Lord. Did You really make them that way on purpose? I hope they will keep out of sight or my womenfolk will be terrified," said Noah still smiling to himself as he went on down the ramp. Before he reached the ground, he almost lost his balance trying to avoid a pair of badgers that scurried past him.

"They must feel it too, Lord... the hurry, I mean. It's getting to be quite a parade. Protect them Lord."

Noah's mind was filled with all that still remained to be done. He must choose seven pair of his best cattle to take into the ark. That would make a good start for the new herd.

"Help me to know which ones to choose, Lord. I'm really not sure which is best. And how can I choose some and leave others. You said only seven pair but it is hard Lord. And the flock Lord. How can I leave the rest of them to die? It will hurt Japheth so much, and he has already known sorrow. You will just have to choose for us some way. You will have to help us with this. You know the end from the beginning. Guide our thoughts and steps. We can do nothing without You."

When Noah reached the house, Evalith was in the central room, preparing the food for the mid-day meal. The girls were still out picking the last of the grapes.

"Any change in Grandfather?"

"No, not much. He is a little more awake, I think."

"I'll go and see him before I eat."

Noah stepped quietly into the little room that had been hastily prepared for his grandfather only a few days ago. It had been here that Noah and his wife had cared for his own father, Lamech, until five years ago. Now Grandfather lay in the same bed.

Noah knelt down and took Grandfather's hand in his. At the touch, Grandfather stirred and opened his eyes. There was a look of recognition and the hint of a smile and then the searching look around the room as though expecting someone else.

"It's me, Noah, Grandfather. Lomar has sent you to me and I am so glad to bid you welcome to my home. It is an honor to have you here."

At the name Lomar, a look of distress spread over Methuselah's face and he tried to speak, but his tongue would not obey and no intelligible words would come. Tears began to flow freely down his face as he shook his head in frustration.

"Do you wish to see Lomar? I can send one of the boys to fetch him."

This suggestion was met with a more vigorous shake of the head and sounds that seemed to be "No. No. No."

"Here, let me help you drink a bit. It will moisten your lips and comfort your throat. There, that's better. Don't worry that you cannot speak. Perhaps in a day or two, you speech will return. Only rest now."

But something was strong on the old man's mind and he gripped Noah's hand and struggled to speak.

"Murmmmm? Muimmmmmm?"

Noah listened and tried to think what he might be asking. What was the name of Lomar's girl who had cared for Grandfather during these last years? He would have to ask Evalith if she remembered.

Going to the door of the kitchen, Noah asked and received an immediate answer. She always remembers names, he thought as he turned back to the bed.

"Were you asking about Miriam? You mean the daughter of Lomar? No I have not seen her. Is she missing?"

Grandfather lay back then, the tears still flowing freely. He nodded to Noah's question and then placed his bony finger against Noah's chest, trying to speak. Then he pointed upward. Again he repeated this gesture, pointing first to Noah and then up.

"You are worried about Miriam and you want me to pray for her?"

Grandfather nodded and lay back, closing his eyes.

Noah hardly knew how to pray. Apparently something serious had happened and Miriam was missing. Perhaps the Nephilim had taken her. Perhaps that same gang of boys that had attacked Rhoda had caught her alone and unprotected. God forbid that it should be that.

"Lord God, together we come to you in behalf of the girl Miriam. You know where she is. Lord protect her. Keep her safe. Put your angels around her and don't let anyone touch her. Take her safely back to her father's house."

This last phrase brought a murmur from Methuselah and he rolled his head from side to side. Then he raised his hand

and pointed down, struggling with the word that would not come.

Noah watched him, trying to read his thoughts. At last he said, "Here? We should ask God to bring her here?"

From the bed came a long sigh and a brief nod.

Noah continued his prayer.

"Bring her to us here if that is what is best. You know where she is. We put her in your hands."

Evalith came in carrying a small bowl of warm broth. Noah moved aside as she knelt down and began to drop a few drops at a time into Grandfather's mouth. Slowly and carefully she worked, giving time for the difficult task of swallowing. Often, in his last days, she had done this for Lamech. Noah watched a moment and then went to see if the boys were coming. Japheth was near the cistern, filling a large clay jar with water.

"I'm taking this into the ark so that the tigers will not have to come out for water," he said. "I don't want to begin using what we have stored there until we need to."

"That is a good idea," his father responded. "I saw bears, wart hogs and badgers come in this morning. We will soon have to sort the cattle, sheep and goats to take, but we must first clip the wool of the whole flock."

"We should finish the grain this evening," Ham said as he came up the path from the field. "We can begin the clipping tomorrow."

"Good. I will not really rest now until we are all in the ark." Noah looked at Japheth as he spoke, wondering how to solve the problem that remained of where to find a wife for this son.

"If only we could get some men to work for us, we could finish everything much faster," put in Shem, who had just walked up the path, "but someone has threatened them if they come near us. Yet all these years we have treated them fairly and paid them well. I really thought some of them would stay."

NO WAY OUT BUT IN

"Don't blame them too much, Shem," said Noah. "Violence and money are very powerful weapons and the authorities have used both to make sure we are isolated. But God is with us. He will not leave us as long as we go on trusting Him."

"Shall we wait for Japheth before we eat?" asked Shem.

"No, he will get involved with his tigers and forget to come back," Ham said with a grin. "I'm hungry. Let's eat!"

Chapter Four

As Miriam gradually came awake, she found herself in a comfortable nest of straw, with a dim light coming from above. It took her a few moments to remember the terrors of the previous night that had crowded her to this place. She wondered what time it was. She must have slept long, after the whole night of walking. She felt around her and found her small bag of belongings. Yes, there was still some fruit. That would ease her hunger and thirst. But what to do next? She had no idea where she was or whether she was safe to remain here.

As she lay back, savoring the sweet juice of the orange, she heard a sound, not far away. It sounded like a dog lapping water. Then a man's voice talking in such low tones that she could not make out any words.

Fear came back in a rush as she realized that she was not alone in this place. She froze, knowing that the slightest movement in this straw might be heard and investigated. The low voice went on for some time but she heard no answering voice—only the lapping of water again and then retreating footsteps.

Miriam finished the orange and slowly ate a dried fig. She checked her bag again and was relieved to see that she still had two flat loaves of bread and a little cheese. She broke off a bit of bread and chewed it slowly, feeling strength beginning to flow back into her aching legs. When the silence beyond the wall grew reassuringly long, she carefully began to crawl towards the side of the high-walled box in which she seemed to be. If she could reach the top and pull herself up, maybe she could tell where she was and which way she should go from here. She had lost all sense of direction during her long night of moving first one way and then another through the labyrinth of streets, but in daylight she might be able to get her directions again.

When she reached the wall, she found that pieces of wood had been fastened to the upright beams, making a kind of a ladder. Carefully pulling herself up, she reached the top and looked around her. Below was a long corridor that led to the open door through which she had entered last night. She looked down to see where the water was that she had heard being lapped. There near the foot of the ladder stood a large earthenware jar, but beside it lay two enormous tigers, calmly licking their paws and washing their faces. Her sudden intake of breath was no more than a whisper but at the sound, both tigers paused in their face washing and looked up at her.

The only time she had ever seen a tiger was that awful day in her father's garden, when a beast like this had exploded from the bushes in front of her and sailed over her head. Her father had taught her to respect and appreciate animals but she had never encountered any like this. She had only seen their coats for sale in the market. She had no way of knowing whether they were safe or dangerous but as she remembered the bandaged face and arm of Koruz, she feared they might be the latter. Had they grown fierce because of all the hunting that was being done? Grandfather had told her the beasts were all tame when he was a young boy and none would harm you if they were not frightened. Still, these were so big. She hoped they would not come near her but at the same time found herself longing to touch their beautiful fur.

Looking again at the door, she could see that the only way to get there was to go past the tigers. This seemed too much to risk so she settled herself to wait. Perhaps they would go away. She watched the door, fearful lest someone would come in and see her there. But instead of people, through the door came a most astonishing parade of small animals: rabbits, squirrels, mice, conies and even some birds. What could bring them into this strange building? No one seemed to be driving them. They simply came. While she stood wondering at this unusual behavior, she heard heavy footsteps on the ramp beyond the door. She let herself down so only her eyes and the top of her head was above the wall. One by one, three men came through the door, burdened down under enormous loads of sheaves bundled up in lengths of sacking. They did not look up but moved below her to another ladder further down the corridor.

Instead of trying to climb the ladder with their loads, they set them down and attached a rope. One of the men quickly climbed the ladder with the rope and pulled the heavy bundles up after him, one after the other. Realizing that this man could now see her, if he happened to look her way, Miriam slowly lowered herself to the bed of straw and waited. She was glad for the dimness of the light. She looked up at the roof above her. It was black, seeming to mute any light that came in from the sides. Because of this, she could not see the men distinctly and she felt certain they had not noticed her. She would wait until they left and then perhaps she could slip out.

The men had not seemed alarmed or surprised to see the tigers there. They must not be very dangerous for they had only watched the men pass and then had gone back to their grooming.

Her mind returned to the perplexing question of how to find the home of Noah without being seen. Ordinarily she could have asked directions on the way, but now Koruz had spread the word that she was to be found and brought to him. She must trust no one but Noah and yet, how could she bring such trouble to his house. He could be killed just like her father had been, if it was learned that she was there.

Oh God, I still don't know what to do. I don't know where I am and I don't know what to do. Help me!

She suddenly remembered that in the terror of last night's journey, she had asked God to show her a place to rest and somehow He had done it. Here she was in a quiet place where she could rest at least for the moment.

But it was my own fear that caused me to come in here last night, my fear and that strange animal that seemed to be following me. Or was it? Could that have been God's way of directing me here? Oh I am so confused. I wish I could talk to Grandfather. She listened to the rustling of the grain sheaves being spread out to dry on the floor now above and beyond her. She heard two sets of footsteps move down the corridor and sound hollowly on the ramp outside. It wasn't long before the third man, apparently finished his task and went down the ladder and out the door, pausing only long enough to say a low word or two to the tigers.

Before she could get up courage to climb the wall again, the men returned with more grain. This went on until the light grew even dimmer and Miriam knew that evening had come. There had been almost no talk among the men all afternoon but now the one spreading the grain called to the others.

"You go on ahead. I'll be there as soon as I've checked the animals."

"Don't take too long, or there may not be any supper left," another voice replied.

In a few minutes, Miriam heard him make his way down the ladder and come to a place just beyond the wall from where she lay. There he paused.

"Well, my beauties, have you had anything to eat today? I brought you a treat here. Some for each of you. Here, now! You couldn't have even tasted that the way you gulped it down. But don't worry, there's plenty more where that came from. Just don't go out and wander around tonight. Koruz has his men watching for you, you know. I'd rather see you wearing those coats that one of Koruz's many wives."

Then his steps moved on down the corridor and soon Miriam could no longer hear them. It didn't seem that he went down the outside ramp, so she waited, almost holding her breath. Soon she heard him return and go down the noisy ramp.

So Koruz was looking for the tigers as well as for her. This made her feel a kinship for them as she thought of their shared enemy. He would destroy them as carelessly as he had her father. He would destroy her, too, if he could. She thought of her mother and sister. She knew her sister well enough to guess that she went with Koruz willingly, thinking only of his handsome face and powerful frame. She always wanted an exciting life. She had been impatient for her marriage for several years now but since she had to wait, being the younger of the two, her dreams had been long delayed. Her father had felt that Grandfather would soon be gone and then he could arrange the marriages. But Grandfather had lived long, longer than anyone. Tired of hearing Leah complain and her mother nag, he had planned her marriage to Laban. She wondered if Leah was happy to be carried away like that. She probably thought it was romantic. Why were they so different, she wondered?

But her mother could not be happy. Poor Mother, torn from her home and having her husband murdered before her eyes. She was not even allowed to grieve and see him properly buried next to his grandfather. Miriam sighed.

"Maybe if I just went out and let Koruz find me, then he would let my mother go back home. Grandfather said it was my father's decision, but now he's gone. And Grandfather is probably gone too."

The thought filled her with such pain that a torrent of weeping overwhelmed her, weeping for her father, for her mother, for Grandfather, for herself.

"Oh God, it hurts so much. Help me! Show me what to do. I need you!" she cried.

Deep racking sobs shook her as all the grief that had been held back by her fear poured out of her. Vividly she could still see her father's face and hear his last words to her. She thought of Grandfather with his long white hair and beard, his dear face wrinkled and old yet with a special light in his eyes. His eyes had always encouraged her, as though she were important to him and he cared to know her thoughts. Now he was gone too. This thought brought a new pain and more tears until her head ached and her tired mind could think no more.

So deep was her grief that she didn't hear the tiger at all until it dropped into the straw beside her. She gave a stifled scream and drew away, but the tiger moved closer and reached out a large red tongue and gently licked away the tears, first from her hands and then from her face. It was a most unusual sensation and not altogether pleasant. Miriam drew a shaky breath, uncertain, and yet strangely comforted by this great beast. It was almost as though this animal had come because of her crying. It seemed, as it looked at her with its great golden eyes, to somehow care that she was sad. As her sobs gradually subsided, the tiger looked up and then gave a great sigh and lay down beside her. Almost immediately the second tiger dropped with a gentle thump onto the straw. The two seemed to commune for a moment with noses touching and a brief mutual face washing and then settled peacefully into the nest beside her.

Miriam sat quietly thinking. Now, for the first time today, she could move out of this place without being seen and without the unknown dangers of the tigers blocking her path. But now she was not sure she wanted to leave. If the tigers were safe from Koruz here, maybe she was too. She began to feel a tiny hope begin to rise in her heart that God had really heard her cry for help last night and had brought her here. She wanted to believe it but it seemed too good to really be true after all that had happened these past two weeks.

Into her troubled mind came quiet words, so quiet that she knew they were not audible. Yet she heard them. "Be still and know the goodness of the Lord."

She wondered if it was something she had heard Grandfather say. It didn't seem to be. Still it seemed like something he would say. He often said that we must trust God. Being still seemed a good way to do that.

In a voice still jerked by leftover sobs, she whispered, "God, I'll just be still now to see your goodness. It is all I can do. I don't know which way to go if I go out. So I'll just be still and wait."

The warmth of the tigers and their even breathing caused her to begin to feel drowsy, but suddenly she realized how very thirsty she was and that there was water close by. She carefully climbed the ladder, and then down the one on the outside of the wall. At the large stone jar she drank deeply until truly satisfied. "You even brought me water," she thought. "Thank you God."

She slipped down the now darkened ramp and out into the night for a few moments to relieve what had become an urgent need. As she came out from beneath the ramp she stood listening to the quiet noises of the night. Far across the fields she could see the lights of a house. There would be people there—and food—but there also might be great danger. Around her feet there seemed to be more small creatures scurrying towards the ramp. Stepping carefully, grateful for a place to go, she once again entered this strange building and found food and a place of comfort and rest between two tigers.

Chapter Five

Noah watched his boys as they came up the path from storing the last of the grain in the ark. One more job done. One day nearer to the impending judgment, which God had assured him, was about to fall. His trip to the market for a sharpening stone to use on the shearing blades had not been pleasant. As he approached the busy stalls, hung about with all manner of woven baskets, leather containers, pottery jars, ropes, and tools all mixed with the pungent aromas of food being prepared and the rhythmic thump of grain being pounded, he saw a knot of men talking excitedly. As he came nearer one of the crowd saw him and shouted, "Noah, have you heard the good news. Koruz has offered a reward for some blond that has escaped him. They say he needs her to complete his collection." Shouts of laughter and lewd comments followed.

Noah ignored the men and began looking through the sharpening stones that were spread on a dirty cloth on the ground. Yes, it was there, just as he had suspected. It bore his own mark but there would be no point in making an accusation. He would simply buy it back with the dried raisins in his bag. He pointed to the stone and the shopkeeper laid it on the bench at the side of the stall. Noah drew out a tightly packed cake of raisins about the width of his hand and laid it beside the stone. The shopkeeper held up two fingers. Noah laid a second cake on the first and picked up the stone. It was wrong to have to buy back his own stone in this way, and he could have made the journey to the place where the stones were found but he didn't feel he had time for either the trip or the argument. God would judge them soon enough.

He could not help hearing the excited talk about Koruz but he paid little attention until he heard the name Miriam mentioned.

"Could it be that it is Miriam, the daughter of my brother, that is being hunted?" he asked the shopkeeper.

"Yes, he claims she was betrothed to him but ran away before the wedding could be held. Stupid girl. Doesn't she know that he will find her in the end? You can't hide from Koruz," replied the rotund little merchant, wiping his dirty hands on his even dirtier robe and sampling a mouthful of the raisins.

"She'll bring punishment down on all of us if she is not found and brought to him," put in a big man who had a pack of wooden pounding pestles on his shoulder. "Who does she think she is to run away from Koruz? She probably thinks she's too 'holy' for the likes of him. Wants some man all to herself, most likely."

Pain filled Noah's heart as he listened and when he could keep silence no longer he spoke to those around him.

"What are you saying? Has not Koruz enough wives already? Must he have another, whether she is pleased to join him or not? Koruz is not God that he must be pleased at all costs! You are afraid of the wrong person. There is a God in heaven who sees what you do. He is not pleased and He has sent me to warn you that He will bring death and destruction on all of you if you continue as you are. You are fearing the wrath of Koruz when you should be fearing the wrath of God!"

"Shut up, old man! We don't want to listen to you any more," shouted one. "Go play with your boat, and leave us alone."

"Maybe you're hiding that girl in your home. Maybe we should tell Koruz to come and ask you about her."

A crowd gathered quickly at the sound of raised voices and it was only with the Lord's strong hand that he was able to push his way through them and bring home his purchase. Filthy words and some stones were thrown after him as he walked away.

"Oh God, my spirit is grieved by such talk. How much more is Yours! Wherever the girl is, protect her. Cover her with your hand so they will not see her," he prayed as he walked home.

He felt dirty after all the vile and unloving talk he had heard. A vigorous wash did little to make his soul feel cleaner. He finished just as the boys came to wash the dust and chaff from their tired bodies. There was little talk until they had gathered around the table for the evening meal.

"God, we give you our thanks for this good food you have provided. Thank you for the good harvest and strength to bring it in. Protect it and all that are in the ark tonight. We are in your hands Lord. Shelter us this night," prayed Noah as they sat down.

Evalith had taken some of the new grain and pounded it and cooked it with some of the raisins that were waiting to be carried into the ark. It made a tasty and filling main dish for the family.

"Grandfather was able to taste a little of the porridge this evening but he still cannot speak so I can understand," commented Evalith. "He still looks for Miriam every time I come in. I wondered what happened?"

"Do you want me to go there to Lomar's house tonight and see what I can find out from him?" asked Shem as he made short work of his porridge.

"I suggested that to Grandfather this morning but it seemed to upset him greatly. Maybe we should wait another day or two. Perhaps the Lord will bring her to us," replied his father. "There was even talk about Miriam in the market this afternoon when I was there. It seems there is a large reward offered to anyone who will bring her to Koruz. They talk as though she is the evil one to be avoiding him."

"But maybe she's not avoiding him. Maybe she is hurt or even dead by now. You know how it is for any girl to be caught out alone now," said Japheth sadly.

There was a pause all around the table as they remembered the beautiful Rhoda.

"I pray that may not be so," said Deborah quietly and there was a murmur of assent.

As the meal finished, they joined hands around the table and sang a hymn of praise to God. This song had come down in the family from Adam who said the tune seemed to echo in the garden each evening during those wonderful days before they disobeyed the Lord. He said it was like it was imbedded in every tree and stone and living creature and their hearts could hear it even though their ears could not. During the moment of silence that followed the hauntingly beautiful song, a call was heard at the front gate. Shem went to answer it and came back with the older son of Lomar.

"Welcome my nephew!" called Noah, rising to meet him when he saw who it was. "We were speaking of your father only a few moments ago and now you are here. Is he well? Oh, but excuse my manners. First come and take some of our new grain just harvested today."

"Thanks Uncle. It's a long walk and I haven't taken my evening meal yet."

"Quickly Deborah! Bring some drink for Cabal and some more of the porridge. There is plenty of fruit here also. Please refresh yourself with this warm towel. We have not seen you for many months and we are anxious for news of your family."

Cabal slowly washed his face and hands with the warm wet towel that was offered. Then after glancing around the room he began to eat.

"I have come to see how Grandfather is," he said hesitantly. "Is he well? Did the servants bring him to you safely?"

"He is well," said Noah, "although he is unable to speak. Has he been that way for very long?"

"No!" Cabal exclaimed, looking truly surprised. "No, he had no problem speaking when he left our place. Has he not talked to you at all since he got here?" Cabal asked with some relief showing in his face even though his words sounded concerned. "He must have suffered a stroke from the journey or maybe it is just that his time has come."

"Why did Lomar send him just now, Cabal?" asked Noah. "Has there been trouble at your home? Is Lomar all right?"

Cabal continued eating for what seemed like a long time and then looked around the room as though afraid someone might be listening. Finally, without meeting his uncle's eyes, he said, "He's dead. He died a week ago or more."

"Dead! Lomar is dead? Why did you not bring us word? We should have been there with you," began Noah. "Was he ill? The servants who brought Grandfather said nothing of this!"

"Yes, he died very suddenly and Koruz thought it best to bury him quietly lest the people be afraid. You see," he paused and cleared his throat, "he was killed by a tiger that has been seen around. Koruz was there and tried to protect him and was also injured. He took care of everything and asked us not to speak of it in the market place."

"I am very sorry to hear this dreadful news, Cabal," Noah said, quickly cutting off Japheth before he could rise in defense of his beloved tigers.

"We felt that Grandfather would be better off here with you, since Miriam disappeared about that time so she was not there to take care of him," Cabal said, pushing back his bowl for another helping. "Has she come here by any chance?"

"No, we have not seen her. Why did she go away from home? Surely she would not leave Grandfather without strong reason."

"Well, her marriage was being planned and she became stubborn about it. She said she wanted to stay with Grandfather. You know how women are sometimes. She is very stubborn but if she comes here, please bring her to us so that the arrangements can be completed."

Japheth started to speak but Noah quieted him with a slight shake of the head. There was more in this than was being said and Noah had long been accustomed to reading people instead of simply accepting their words. Words could be deceptive but people found it hard to hide their true thoughts. Noah studied Cabal quietly for some minutes. Finally he said quietly, "It is strange that she would run away, if her desire was to stay with Grandfather. And surely if the tiger is dangerous, people should be warned. It seems a strange course to try to hide such a thing."

"Did you see this attack happen?" asked Shem, taking his cue from his father.

"Yes I was there. It was a terrible experience and I don't like to even think about it. Please, I'd just rather not talk of it, if you don't mind."

"Very well, Cabal. I can respect your feelings. But I must remind you of what God has said. Very soon now, He will destroy all living things on the earth in a great flood because of the great wickedness of men. You are a son of my youngest brother. Since he is gone, I feel responsible for you. I beg of you to come and join us in preparing for this judgment. There is no need for you to perish with the others. There is room for you in the ark with us. Please bring your mother and sister and brother as well. You are family. I care what happens to you."

Cabal shifted nervously and glanced briefly at Noah. Then he rose from the table saying, "I'm sorry Uncle. I have obligations to Koruz that I must fulfill. Thank you for your hospitality and your concern. I must be getting home and it is a long way. Please be sure to bring Miriam to us if she comes here, won't you."

"I will remember Cabal. But Miriam will be allowed to choose what she will do. I can only pray that she is still alive. You know how dangerous it is for a woman to be out alone these days. I have heard of the great reward that is being offered for her as though she were some dumb beast to be sold," replied Noah in a voice filled with pain as well as anger.

"Koruz will not be pleased if he finds you are allowing her to live here. I must warn you that he is a man of great power and not to be trifled with. But if you bring her to me, so I can complete the wedding arrangements, he will not harm you."

"But surely you can not plan a wedding when your father is only a week in his grave. That is unthinkable!" sputtered Shem.

"We live in a new age, Shem. Not the old days. We must move with the times. That is the only way to survive these days. If you are wise, you can see that. But I must be going. Thank you again for the meal."

"Do you not wish to see Grandfather before you go?" asked Shem. "I'm sure he would want to see you."

"No, he is probably sleeping now. He always sleeps early. I will see him next time I come."

Shem walked with Cabal to the gate where he took his leave abruptly and walked into the night.

Inside the house, there was a quick rush of talk.

"Father, I simply don't believe that a tiger killed Uncle Lomar. They are gentle beasts unless they are harmed or harried," burst out Japheth, pacing around the room. "Do you believe his story, Father?"

"His words were rather strange and did not seem to match his thoughts. If only Grandfather could talk, we would know what really happened. But this visit only increases my sense of urgency. We must finish our work quickly tomorrow. I had hoped to hire some men to help us, but after my visit to the market, I decided it would be futile to try."

"And we must pray for the girl, Miriam," said Deborah. "She must be in great danger if she is not already dead."

"I wonder if Koruz has sent men to watch our house, thinking she might try to come here," mused Ham. "I think I'll go out and take a look around before I go to bed."

"I'll come with you. I want to carry another jar of water and you can bring a load of the raisins," suggested Japheth. "Shem, why not bring one too. We can get them all in if we make a couple of trips each."

"I'll go in and spend some time with Grandfather," said Noah. "He may have heard Cabal's voice and be feeling concerned. I find it hard to believe that my brother is dead and buried and we have not been informed. Harder still to believe that he would offer his daughter to Koruz freely, or that Cabal would give her to him just for the money. How I wish Grandfather could tell us what really happened."

Carrying a small oil lamp, Noah found Methuselah awake and nervously pulling at the blanket that covered him. Tears rolled freely from the corners of his eyes. His hand trembled as he reached out and drew Noah close to him.

"It is all right, Grandfather. There is no cause to be worried. God is with us and He has not lost His power."

With contorted face, Methuselah tried his best to speak but all that came was a murmur of sound.

"No, there is still no news of Miriam but we will trust our God to protect her. Cabal was just here looking for her. He asked me to send her to him if she comes to us. I made him no promise. We will hear what she says first if she comes. Cabal said that Lomar had arranged a marriage for her with Koruz. Is this true?"

At this Methuselah groaned in protest and slowly rolled his head from side to side.

"I found it hard to believe that he would do that. But did you also know that Lomar is dead?"

There was a nod of assent as Methuselah struggled to bring out a word. When no discernible word would come, fresh tears came instead and a frustrated shaking of the head.

"Never mind, Grandfather. Just rest now. Maybe tomorrow God will find a way to bring Miriam to us. We must go on trusting Him. He is a God who hears and answers prayers. We will pray now and then you sleep. We will talk more of this tomorrow."

In the kitchen, he found Evalith and his two daughters-in-law busy picking dried grapes from their stems and pressing them into cakes. These were almost the last of the crop. Noah looked at them and wondered when they would again be able to harvest. He had already taken cuttings into the ark, so they could be planted once the flood was past.

"Was Grandfather awake when you went in?" asked Deborah.

"Yes, and very distressed. He already knew of Lomar's death and tried very hard to tell me about it. But he could only cry."

"Your father was like that in his last days. Remember? He would try so hard to talk and only meaningless sounds would come," mused Evalith. "Strange isn't it. We begin life only being able to cry and we often end life the same way. How I would like to hear him tell one more time of his days with Adam."

"God never intended us to grow old and die. He planned for us to live and grow up to be like Him, wise, loving and creative," Noah said with a heavy sigh. "Instead, we have chosen to grow selfish, cruel and full of hatred. It is only by His mercy that we continue to live at all. And most of the race is polluted with the seed of the Nephilim, which God also never intended. If only they would repent and turn to Him, He would yet have mercy."

Quiet tears began to flow down his strong face, glistening on his beard in the leaping flame of the oil lamp. "Poor Cabal. He would not listen. He and so many like him. Young Cor who grew up among us and worked for us so many years. He left because of fear and riches. So many others," Noah said with a groan. "All my brothers and sisters have turned away from God and their children and grandchildren follow them. Now even Lomar is gone. He was the only one who still held any faith in God. Sometimes I marvel that God has given us three sons who will stand by us, Eva."

"But no grandchildren, Noah. All these years now and no grandchildren," Evalith said a little sharply as though an old wound had been opened.

"Surely God could have given us grandchildren by this time. Shem is nearly 100 years old now and he and Deborah have been married many years. Still her seasons come and go and there is no child."

"Please don't fret, Eva. Remember, how old we were when our sons were born. I believe it is God's mercy that no children have come. The flood will be a hard time for all of us and little ones might not survive. God has promised children and He never lies as men do. It is just that we don't know His timing."

Deborah and Loma shifted uneasily and glanced at each other. They felt somehow to blame that there were no children and yet they felt anger too. Month by month they would hope, only to despair yet again when there was no evidence of quickening life.

"It doesn't seem fair somehow," said Loma with a frown furrowing her usually smooth brow. "At the well I see so many women who laugh at God and do just as they please and they are heavy with child. Yet here we sit, barren," her voice rose. "Do you really think that is God's kindness?" The last word came with a painful hiss.

"Yes, I really do, Loma. God's ways are higher than our ways but He is never needlessly cruel. His judgment is always tempered with mercy. Think how He has waited these one hundred years, giving me time to build and provision the ark for our safety and at the same time, giving people time to repent and turn from their wickedness. He is very patient but He is also righteous. Your children are safe within you until His judgment is past. But these children you see being born now will not be safe. They will all perish if their parents do not repent. Ah, the children... all the children... and the animals!" Noah groaned, burying his face in his rough work-torn hands. "I can not bear to think of all of them. If only I could bring all of them into the ark. But God will permit only those who come willingly."

Deborah sat quietly looking at the fruit in her lap. "It is so very long and I am not so patient as God. And there is the fear too. Every day the town's people become more and more open in their threats against us. Only this morning I heard the women talking. They were saying that the men are making jokes about burning the ark. You know how quickly pitch burns and the town's people have thought of that too."

"Who said that, Deborah?" asked Loma. "I didn't hear anyone talking about that."

"It was after you had started home this morning. I was still filling the jugs and the wife of Luz was talking to Mara."

Evalith looked quickly at Noah, the worry line growing deep between her large dark eyes.

"Noah, what will we do if that happens? There is no way we could start over again. Everything that we will ever have is in that ark. All our food, all your crops, all the labor of a lifetime. It could all be gone in one night!" Evalith said, jumping up. "What could we do?"

"Now, now, don't be alarmed. I have heard such talk before but God is our protector. He will cover us with His hand and no one can touch us. They wanted to attack me in the market this morning, but He did not let them touch me. I don't understand how, but I trust Him and you don't need to worry, Eva. He is greater than any fire."

The three women looked at each other as they stacked the raisin cakes on the table and covered them with a clean cloth. It was plain to see that they were not convinced even though they said no more. Noah moved to the door to see if the boys were coming back.

"Protect the ark tonight, Lord, and all that is within it," murmured Noah. "Protect us too. Comfort the women and give them courage to face this great trial. Send us the wife that Japheth needs, Lord. Keep her pure and keep her safe tonight wherever she is. Help us tomorrow as we gather the wool. We are few and the flock is prone to drift now that the men have gone away. Help us to gather it and get the wool that we will need. Help us to choose from the flock and herd those that will be strong for the future. You are a God who even cares about the animals.

"I pray for Cabal and the rest of his family. Have mercy on them. Turn them from their wicked way. Surely you can turn their hearts to do Your will. Your mercy is great and new every morning. Lomar was my youngest brother, Lord. I am responsible for his children. For the girl Miriam, help her if she is still alive. Bring her to me Lord if this is your plan. She also is a child of my brother. Grandfather is so concerned for her. Give him peace in these his last days. He has always been our remembrancer and now he cannot even speak. Help him, Lord. May his soul depart peacefully.

"Help me Lord. My soul is very weary with the pressure of wickedness all around me. Keep me loving in the face of hatred. Keep me strong in You for You are my hiding place. I have no one to turn to but You. Hear my voice when I call, oh Lord, and be merciful and answer me. One word from You is sweeter than ten thousand words from anyone else. I am so troubled that I can hardly hear You. Speak loudly Lord so that I do not make a mistake. I feel the heavy weight of this task. If, even now, You can turn aside Your judgment, I pray that it might be so. Nothing is impossible with You, Lord. Yet I accept Your Way. You know what is best."

Chapter Six

The next morning, Noah and his three sons set out on donkeys to the pasture near the mountain slope where their sheep and cattle grazed in a natural bowl, one end of which reached right to the base of the mountain itself. From beneath this mountain wall flowed a wide deep stream of clear, cold water. Because of this, none of the herds strayed far outside the long green valley that nestled between the foothills.

When they reached the brow of the hill overlooking the valley they could see the livestock quietly feeding. Each man carried wool clippers and stout cord with which they could tie the fleeces. The animals showed no fear of them and they spread out through the flock, quietly catching the unresisting sheep and clipping them quickly. The longhaired goats were more prone to struggle but even they did not run away when they were approached. The men worked steadily through the morning and by noon they had more than the donkeys could carry in one trip.

"I'll take this load back to the ark, while you go on clipping," suggested Shem. "I can get back before sundown and that way we can get all the wool in today."

"It is good," said Noah. "You can make the trip faster than I and I don't look forward to two trips in one day. You'd better take some of the food with you and eat it on the way."

Shem loaded the donkeys, took one long last drink from the spring and started back.

Noah moved down to the edge of the stream and sat down under a great spreading tree that stood with its toes in the water. The spring flowed smoothly and although it was several feet deep, Noah could clearly see the stones on the bottom. After a leisurely meal, as he knelt to drink, he felt suddenly dizzy and off balance. He lifted himself quickly and was surprised to see the whole surface of the water was disturbed, dimpled and roughened strangely but not with waves or circles. He quickly glanced around him and was surprised to see every animal was alert, ears straining and some were running about for no apparent reason. On the mountainside above him, small stones were rolling and many pieces splashed into the stream near the wall. The boys were looking about with puzzled faces. The dizziness that he had felt was gone now.

"Lord God, we are in your hands. Show me what I need to know about this strange occurrence. This is your world to do with as you will," he said quietly.

Ham and Japheth came quickly over.

"Did you feel that, Father?" began Ham. "It was is if the whole earth moved under us!"

"I thought it was only that I was dizzy from the sun and heat until I looked at the animals," Japheth said excitedly. "Can the earth really shake under us like that?"

"I do not know," answered Noah, "but even the water was disturbed. God will tell us what we need to know about it. See the animals are beginning to feed again. Let's finish the shearing and be ready when Shem returns."

"Should we take the animals back with us to the ark today?" asked Ham.

"Yes, if we can finish soon enough. I feel great urgency to hurry. We must choose young animals. Perhaps yearlings will be best. We may have trouble getting them to leave this place because the food and water are plentiful and they will not want to leave the herd either."

Through the afternoon they worked and were just finishing as Shem came over the shoulder of the foothill to the west.

"It is too late to sort and drive the animals now. We will have to come back for them tomorrow," Noah said.

In the ark, Miriam had been awakened early by the movement of the hay as the tigers launched themselves to the top of the wall and dropped from sight on the other side. She followed them up the ladder and was soon standing beside the water tub drinking and then wetting the ends of her long sleeves to use as a face cloth. No men approached all day and Miriam had taken her courage in hand and explored a bit to see what strange building this might be. It seemed that everywhere she looked there was food, all kinds of food. Being very hungry, she took a bit here and a bit there so that nothing would be noticeably missing.

"Is it stealing, God? I don't want to take what belongs to someone else, but you seem to have provided it. Grandfather always said we should take what You provide and be thankful. And I am very thankful.

"I wonder where my mother is. Is she happy? And silly Leah who always wanted adventure. Is she pleased to be in the house of Koruz? How can I find Uncle Noah? Grandfather said I was to go to him but I am afraid to ask anyone where he is or even where I am. If I had gone around the city, I would have recognized the way, but coming through all those streets that twisted and turned, I don't even know which direction to go."

Miriam was sitting now on the upper floor where the sweet smell of fresh unthreshed grain comforted her. She rolled a handful of grain between her palms to free the kernels and ate them slowly, savoring their fresh nutty goodness. The light came from above somehow and filled the huge long room with muted light. She had been surprised to find that in the middle of the building was a open sort of aisle that seemed to go clear to the ground. During the day, the light shone down so that even the lowest part of the building was not really dark. But there were many rooms and stalls and bins and more food than she could imagine. Could this be some great storehouse of Koruz? He was always building and making. Her brother had said he was even planning to bring the river through the city so that people would have plenty of water without digging wells.

Suddenly from outside, Miriam heard voices of several men approaching and she quickly dropped down into her nest and put a trembling hand on the back of one of the tigers, which was now lying there.

As the footsteps came up the ramp, one of the men said, "Did you ask permission at the house to search this building?"

"No. What's the use? Koruz told us to search every building and even if they said no, we would have to do it anyhow. Let's just get on with it."

"I don't like the look of it much. It's so big and black and who knows what may be inside," came a third voice.

"Are you scared? If you're scared, just wait outside. We don't need any yellow-bellied insects tagging along," snarled the leading man with a curse.

"I ain't scared! But I just think we ought to have someone on the ramp in case anybody comes up behind us."

Miriam could hear the anger in their voices and their curses that punctuated every sentence fell roughly on her ears. She had been so sheltered in her father's house. She had never had to listen to the men of the city as they went about their business. She crouched down and covered her ears, as the quarrel beyond the wall grew more violent.

Suddenly, around her there arose a strange wave of noise; it seemed to be a roar like a great wind, mingling with the animal and bird voices all talking at once. Birds which were perching in the rafters above began flying around and the tigers which had been lying quietly in the straw at her side scrambled up suddenly, ears alert and tails twitching. Then beneath her she felt the boards tremble and shake as though some strong hand was shaking the entire building.

Below in the passage, the men grew suddenly quiet and Miriam lay frozen in terror, as she sent a wordless cry to God.

"What's going on anyway?" said one of the men in a half whisper.

As suddenly as the shaking had started, it was over, leaving only the cries and fluttering of the birds above.

"How should I know?" growled the first man. "It felt like the whole wretched building moved. Anyway, it seems to be over so let's get on with this. You go that way and I'll go this. It's not very light in here but our eyes will soon get used to it."

As one set of footsteps neared the wall below her, Miriam heard once again the quick little hard hooves of that strange pig-like animal that had frightened her so much the first night. It came clattering up from the lower level and Miriam could imagine it waving its long snout from side to side as it grunted menacingly. There was a shout from one of the men and hurried scurry of steps.

"Do you see that thing that came up from down below? Look! It doesn't look very friendly."

"It's a wart-hog, I think. What's it doing in here anyway?"

"Shoo! Get away! I should have brought my knife."

The two men stood staring at the animal that had stopped just short of the ramp. Then behind them came a loud snuffling snort. The black bears that had been aroused by the trembling, stood peering near-sightedly at the two men. Their wide bodies effectively blocked the passage beside Miriam's hiding place. At that moment, from deep in the belly of the building, two wolves that had only arrived the day before, lifted their noses and howled their mournful cry that echoed through the passageways in what seemed like a lament for an entire world of pain.

Shouting curses at each other and the animals, the men made a break for the ramp and Miriam listened with relief to their hurried exit, apparently followed by that persistent strange hog.

"What will we tell Koruz?" she heard one of them say.

"We'll tell him we looked and didn't see the girl anywhere. That's the truth. You know how he can tell if you're lying."

Fresh fear welled up inside Miriam as the import of their words became clear.

"They were looking for me!" whispered Miriam as she huddled lower in the straw. "They will come back. Koruz will send them back. I know he will. Oh God, cover me with Your hand. Don't let them find me here."

The minutes stretched into an hour. The tigers finally stretched out and began to groom themselves and the knot had just begun to loosen in Miriam's stomach when more footsteps came up the ramp. She heard a man's voice seemingly talking to his donkeys and after several trips in and out of the building, she heard him move away with them.

In the stillness, the memory of her father's last moments replayed through her mind again and again. Waves of pain and grief washed over her. *Why did Father have to die? Why did God let all this happen? Grandfather had always said*

*that God loves us and that He can hear our prayers. The
more I pray, the worse things get.*

She could see no way for life to ever be good again. Her
father was gone; her mother was gone; her home was no
longer a safe haven; her brothers would not, or could not
help her, Grandfather was gone and she was all alone.

Have you gone away too, God? Do you care at all? As
a fresh torrent of deep sobs racked her slender body, once
again the tiger reached out and gently licked away her tears
with his large red tongue but even this gentle gesture failed to
reach her, so low had she sunk in the blackness of despair.

At last, worn out by the fear and grief, Miriam dropped
into an exhausted sleep and when she awakened, it was dark
and empty around her. Beyond the wall, she could hear a
gentle voice, once again talking to the tigers.

"Well, my beauties, I'm glad to see you are still here. I
was afraid Koruz might have found you today. Mother said
his men came to search this place. How did you manage to
elude them?"

There was a loud snuffling snort in the passageway
below.

"So, look who is jealous and wants an ear scratch as well.
You bears are so black; you look like part of the wall. Here
are some dried figs. You don't look like you need them, as
fat as you are."

Miriam listened to the kind voice and thought it sounded
faintly like Grandfather. It was not so much the sound as the
gentleness and the warmth. Could this be one of Noah's sons?
A flicker of hope sprang up in her mind and then died with the
thought that even if this was Uncle Noah's place, her presence could bring death to them all just as it had to her father.
An overwhelming longing swept over her to tell someone all
that had happened during these past two weeks. Ever since
that last brief talk with Grandfather, she had spoken to no

one — no one but God and the tigers. Oh how she needed to talk to someone!

"Go to Noah," Grandfather had said. But the risk was too great.

The next morning, although all was quiet in this great dark building, Miriam did not move far from her hiding place. She listened intently for a return of those men who had been sent to search for her, knowing that Koruz would ferret the truth from them and send them back.

It was nearing noon when once again the animals in the ark began to stir and pace. The monkeys that had arrived last night started screeching and the same eerie howls erupted from deep in the ark. Then she heard the rumbling. It seemed to come marching across the land and as the source of the noise came close, the whole building began to shake and tremble. Miriam was knocked off her feet as she tried to stand. The building beams groaned and creaked. Then as suddenly as it had started, it was past.

Miriam sat still, fear welling up in her throat until it almost choked her. Was this some terrible deed of Koruz, to cause her to run out of her hiding place? What could shake the whole building? It seemed that the very earth had moved. She had never experienced anything like it before and on top of her already fearful heart, it seemed unbearable.

Then she heard men coming. There were shouts and whistles and the sound of running animals. As they came near, Miriam could hear the lowing of cattle and the bleating of the sheep. Hard hooves thundered on the ramp as the cattle pushed and jostled their way into the building and down the passageway below her. After them came the men, and a small flock of sheep.

"Can you believe that? They came right in, in spite of the earthquake. I thought they would scatter every which way," came one excited voice.

"They looked like they knew where they were going. We could barely keep up with them, especially after that shaking started," came another excitement- filled voice. "That was much stronger than yesterday."

"We'll have to bring in more water," said a voice Miriam had heard before. It was the kind voice that talked to the tigers. "They will be really thirsty after that run."

"Maybe we should drive them back out to the watering trough beside the cistern."

"No!" an older voice carried great authority. "God has sent them inside today. We couldn't have done this all alone. God has sent them to us. Didn't you see how just the right number separated themselves from the herd? And how in spite of their leaving the sources of water and food, and the shaking of the earth, they simply came here. Surely God has done this and we must work with Him and not according to our own planning."

Miriam listening behind the wall felt the tears well up from deep inside. They were not tears of grief this time, but tears of relief and wonder. She recognized that voice! It was her uncle, Noah! No one but Uncle Noah would speak of God like that. He sounded so much like Grandfather that she could barely restrain herself from calling out to him. She took a deep breath to shout and then caught herself. Koruz! He would kill Uncle Noah if he found her here. She must not cause this good man's death as she had that of her own father. She sat down quietly so as not to rustle the straw.

The tigers felt no such compunction and launched themselves up and over the wall.

"So. That's where you two sleep, you clever cats," said one of the boys. "Count on you to find the softest bed in the place."

"We'll have time to bring in the extra water and some more of that straw before lunch. Japheth, you get the straw and Ham and I will get the water."

What should I do now? Miriam wondered. *Grandfather said to go to Uncle Noah and in spite of all my wandering, that is what I did.* "Oh God! You did hear my prayer after all. You did show me the way even when I didn't know it. But now what do I do? I could go to Uncle. I could run again. Or I could just continue to hide," she whispered. "Dear God, you brought me to this place of safety and rest. It would be foolish to leave it. Yet I must not let them find me and cause trouble for them. Please God, hide me."

Below her in the passage, she could hear the boys passing and water being poured into the large stone jars that sat at the end of the passage. Then there was a rustling as Japheth came back with a large bundle of hay. He tied it to the rope he had used to lift the bundles of grain to the next level. Miriam listened as his steps climbed the ladder and began dragging the load toward her hiding place. She crouched back in a corner, hoping in the dim light he would not notice her as he passed.

Then new voices could be heard, rough ones that were only too familiar. As they came up the ramp, Shem and Ham moved to meet them. Noah had already gone on to the house.

"What do you want in here?" asked Shem.

"Koruz sent us," said one. "He thinks you are hiding that girl Miriam here and he sent us to get her."

"We have no girl here," said Shem. "We have only animals and birds."

"You can look if you like," put in Ham. "We have nothing to hide."

Above, Japheth continued to drag his load along the floor. Then stooping to untie the rope, he gathered the hay into his arms, glancing quickly into the bin before dropping it there. He found himself looking straight into the frightened eyes of his cousin Miriam. Her hand was covering her mouth as though to stifle a scream as she cowered in the corner below him.

Japheth looked down at the three men who were even then moving toward the ladder of this bin. Quickly he looked back at Miriam and then deliberately dropped the loose hay into the bin, covering her completely.

"Sure, you can look all you want," he called. "We are just putting in our fodder for the cattle we brought in today."

Not daring to breathe, Miriam heard the man on the ladder, just on the other side of the wall against which she was pressed. Then he climbed up beside Japheth and went on to the threshing floor where she could hear him kicking the sheaves about. Japheth stood watching him a few moments and then calmly descended the ladder for another load.

Four times that long hour, Miriam heard Japheth climb that ladder and felt the new loose hay gently fall onto the heap under which she lay. Dust filled her nose and she kept her eyes tightly shut, telling herself that her very life depended on not sneezing. There were twitters and shrieks from the birds and monkeys in the upper level and groans and snorts from the larger animals below, but none seemed to menace the searchers. The tigers lay quietly too, occasionally shaking their heads and washing their whiskers. Noah's sons continued to work quietly in the midst of the search and at last the men left, cursing and swearing as they moved down the plank.

"If Koruz finds that you have deceived him, you are all dead men," the leader of the group flung back over his shoulder. "He will burn this place down if necessary to get that girl!"

The three brothers stood for many minutes in the door, watching them go and then turned back into the ark.

Chapter Seven

"**D**o you think they will be back?" asked Japheth as the brothers moved slowly down the passageway.

"It's hard to say," said Shem, thrusting his work-scarred hand through his thick black beard. "They made a very thorough search but will Koruz believe them? That's the question. Deborah said they were here yesterday but stayed a very short time. It was about the time of the earthquake and maybe they got scared or maybe the animals were so restless that they were frightened by them."

"We've got nothing to hide," put in Ham. "I say let them come. But where were the tigers today? I thought they wanted them too and yet I didn't see them anywhere."

"They have made a nest in that straw bin there," said Japheth, "but they didn't show themselves. All the time I was filling it with straw, they just lay there and shook the straw out of their eyes as it dropped down on them. Of course, with their color, and in the dim light, they just looked like straw too. That one man looked in the bin but failed to see them."

"Well, let's go and have something to eat. All this tension has made me hungry," said Ham, "and we must tell Father about their threat. But let's not talk about it in front of the women. You know how they worry."

"You go ahead," said Japheth. "I want to check on the tigers before I come in."

"Don't take too long, or we'll eat all the food," warned Ham with a laugh.

As the two men moved out into the bright sunlight and down the ramp toward the house, Japheth again climbed the ladder of the bin. It was not tigers that drew him but two very frightened blue eyes that he had glimpsed earlier that morning. Why had he not told his brothers? He wasn't sure. Somehow it seemed important to talk to Miriam alone first.

"Miriam," he called softly, "you can come out now. They've all gone. Don't be afraid."

There was a rustling in the straw below him and Miriam's head pushed through the straw. She looked up into his face for a long moment. She had been crying and the dust was smudging her face.

"Come on up, Miriam. You're safe now," Japheth assured her, stretching out his hand to help her up the ladder.

The tigers decided it was their time to leave the nest as well and launched themselves, one after the other, to the top of the bin and then jumped with light thumps to the passageway below. Miriam could hear them lapping water as she shook herself free of the straw and climbed to the top of the box.

Japheth could feel her trembling as he grasped her hand and pulled her up beside him.

"Why didn't you tell us you were here? How long have you been hiding here anyway?"

"I... I'm not quite sure how many days," Miriam answered with a shaky voice, "and I didn't know where I was for sure until yesterday. It was because of me that Father was killed and I didn't want to bring trouble to you too. You heard what they said. They will kill you all if they find me here. I came here during the night about a week ago when I was running from Koruz. I found this place to hide and was afraid to leave it. The tigers seemed to feel it was safe here and I thought maybe it was safe for me as well."

Japheth smiled at the jumbled account. "God must have guided you here," he said quietly.

"You mustn't tell anyone I'm here, Japheth. Not even Uncle Noah or anyone. That way they won't have to lie when Koruz comes the next time. His men said he can tell if you are lying to him. Oh please don't tell anyone! I just couldn't bear to bring death to all of you as I did to my own dear father. Please just let me go away so no one will know where I am."

"No Miriam, I can't do that. Besides Grandfather has been so worried about you and keeps asking for you."

"Grandfather!" Miriam gasped. "Is he alive? Is he here? Oh, I was so sure he was dead too," she sobbed as she collapsed in a heap with all the conflicting emotions swirling about in her mind.

"I must go to Grandfather! He needs me," she began, starting to rise.

No sooner had this glimpse of normality begun to take hold of Miriam's mind when the overwhelming blackness of the real situation reasserted itself.

"But if I do that, you all may die. Oh why must it be so hard to know what is right? Why must everything be the wrong thing to do?"

In Japheth too there arose a surge of conflicting emotions and memories. As he looked at his cousin, in his heart he was remembering his Rhoda. She too had been so beautiful and innocent. Her death was still a living pain and Miriam's distress tore at his own wound. The need to do something to assuage her grief rose strongly in him. He had been so impotent to help his Rhoda. He had not been there when she needed him. He had lived with this bitter fact for two years. Now at least he could do something about this pain before him.

"Come. Let's go down the ladder and get you a cool drink. You must be very thirsty after your morning in the hay. Come. I'll help you."

"But what if those men come back?"

"Let's trust God. Surely He has brought you here. Come. I'm thirsty too. Let's go and get a drink."

It had seemed an eternity since someone had spoken kindly to her and had been concerned for her needs. Miriam brushed the rolling tears away with the back of her hand and got shakily to her feet. Japheth went first and moved quickly to the door to assure himself and Miriam that the men had truly gone.

Then he helped her down the ladder and waited while she dipped water from the large tub with the gourd and drank deeply. Using her long sleeve as a face cloth, she dealt with the dust and chaff and as her clean face emerged from behind all the debris, Japheth smiled.

"Don't you look different." His eyes lingered on her face longer than necessary but Miriam was busy watching the door and didn't notice.

"Grandfather is really alive, and just there in the house?"

"Yes, your brother Cabal sent him here about a week ago. But he must have suffered a stroke because he can't talk. The servants who brought him would tell us nothing. Father was able to understand that he was worried about you but none of the details of what had happened. Then only two days ago, your brother himself came and told us that your father had been killed by the tiger and that Koruz was looking for you. He said you had been promised to Koruz and asked Father to bring you home if you came here. Father did not fully believe him."

"No! Oh no, no, no!" wailed Miriam. "How could he say such a thing? How can he lie like that? It was because Father would not give me to Koruz that Koruz killed him."

Miriam sank to her knees and covered her face as the brutal scene replayed itself again in her mind. Would this nightmare never stop?

Japheth's usually gentle face became grim as he realized the truth of the situation. So Koruz really would kill to have this girl. Perhaps Miriam was right in thinking that her presence endangered them all. But what should he do? Should he continue to hide her and not tell his father and brothers? Could he deny Grandfather the joy of seeing her alive and well? They were both so deep in their own thoughts that neither heard the quiet footsteps that climbed the ramp. Noah stood in the doorway, letting his eyes accustom themselves to the dim passageway before him.

"Japheth? Are you there?" he called quietly and he moved along toward them.

Miriam sprang up and started to run down the aisle but Japheth caught her arm.

"Wait," he said. "God is in this. Let's let Him do it His way."

"Miriam! Is it really you?" exclaimed Noah as he took in the scene before him. He spoke with such joy that Miriam's heart turned over within her. Another kind voice! Maybe Grandfather had been right when he said she should come to this place.

Noah swept the trembling girl into his great strong arms and held her close. "Thank you God! Oh thank you for keeping this child safe and bringing her here to us! You are truly the Living One. The God who hears and answers. We offer up to you our sacrifice of praise."

Then, holding her at arms length Noah looked keenly into her face. There was a moment of silent listening and then with a brief nod he continued. "But my child, you must come and have some food and see your grandfather. He is longing for you so greatly."

"But Uncle, if Koruz finds me here, you may all be killed! It was because of me that Koruz killed my father. He tried to protect me. I am a danger to you."

"So, Koruz was the one who struck down your father. I am not surprised. Well, never mind that. God has said that you are to stay here. He will protect you if He has brought you to us. Do you want to stay with us, Miriam? We welcome you if you do but we will not keep you against your will."

"I could not bear to cause your death, Uncle."

"Of course not, child. But that is not my question. You must know that all men are against me and are under God's judgment because of their sins. If you stay with me, you are saying that you want to go God's way. I cannot force you to do this but I plead with you to accept this place as God's place of safety for you. Please stay with us, Miriam."

"Grandfather told me to come to you, Uncle. I was too afraid at first, then I lost my way crossing the city at night, and then I was chased in here by that strange pig-like thing and didn't know where I was until I heard your voice yesterday. I asked God to lead me, but with everything that had happened I thought maybe Cabal was right. Maybe there wasn't any God who could hear me.

"I'd like to stay. I so want to see Grandfather but surely your servants will talk. Then Koruz will come and if you try to stop him, he will kill you like he did my father. I can not bear that."

Once again the tears came and despair settled like a cloud on Miriam's pale face.

"We have no servants, Miriam. But you are right to want to be careful," Noah said kindly. "It may be best to wait until dark to come to the house. Those men may be watching even now. There is plenty of food for you here. Help yourself to anything you want and when it is dark, I will send Japheth to get you.

"In the mean time be assured that our God is alive and He is in control. Cabal has believed a lie and I cannot persuade him otherwise. But it gives me great joy to welcome you into my family. I will care for you as your own father would wish. You are home now Miriam. Please rest in that reality and don't worry about how God will protect us. He has His ways that are much greater than our ways. We must just trust him.

"Japheth, if the men are watching, they will wonder why you have stayed here so long. Go along into the house and I will follow in a moment. Miriam, climb up to the upper level where you will find food and where you can hide yourself again if necessary. I will see you after it is dark."

Miriam watched as Japheth started toward the doorway but quickly dropped her eyes when he turned and looked back. Noah stood quietly and seemed to be listening. Then his eyes moved quickly to Miriam and a smile came into them.

"Yes, my Lord. I see. You have planned it all the time. I could not see it before," he murmured quietly. And with an encouraging smile, he helped Miriam as she started up the ladder.

The afternoon stretching out before Miriam seemed endless. Her jumbled thoughts moved in circles. How she longed to run quickly to Grandfather's side and yet she must wait until it was safe. He had been right. God did have another plan but it had brought her through such pain... could it really have been His plan? Surely God did not wish her father to be dead and her mother and sister in the house of Koruz. Yet He had guided her here and it was the very place where she wanted to go. She wished she had trusted Him more. It would have saved her a lot of fear.

But even this knowledge did not erase the pain of her father's death. *Does God purposely lead us into pain or is it just that there is no other way to go?* So many questions.

"Grandfather is alive!" She hugged this joyous thought to herself as she ate some figs and chewed a handful of the sweet new wheat. Tonight she would be with him again. Tonight! When her hunger was satisfied, she at last was able to settle back into the new straw in the bin and sleep more deeply than she had for several weeks. Her last thoughts however were not of Grandfather but lingered instead over the kind face of her cousin Japheth.

Chapter Eight

It was doubly dark in the passageway late that night as Miriam stood waiting for Japheth to come and get her. As the afternoon progressed, excitement began to rise in Miriam and now she longed to run to her grandfather. He seemed the one link back to life as she had known it. So silent was Japheth's approach that only the tigers heard him and rose to meet him as he came up the ramp.

"Miriam, are you there?" It was a whisper.

Miriam gave a start. "I'm here, Japheth. I didn't hear you come. Is it safe to go now?"

"If they have men watching, they have been very clever. But we've taken every precaution. Come. I know the way without a light."

Guided by Japheth's hand on her elbow, the two made their way down the ramp and through the field. It was a darkened house that greeted them. No light shown from the windows. It seemed that all were asleep. Japheth pushed the door open carefully and quickly both slipped inside. Through the darkened house he guided her until she stood in a small bedroom. Here the door was carefully covered before the woven basket was taken from the flickering oil lamp. Every window had been covered with black goatskins.

By the light of the lamp, Miriam could see the face of her beloved grandfather. With a stifled sob, she flung herself down beside the low bed and buried her face in her grandfather's shoulder.

"Miriam!" Grandfather gasped, seeing her dear familiar face and then they could only cry for long minutes, silent sobs lest anyone hear them. At last Miriam sat back, still holding Grandfather's frail hands.

"I thought you were dead too, Grandfather," whispered Miriam, brushing away the tears with the back of her hand. "You told me to come here but I was afraid and then you were gone. When I tried to come, I got lost and then God sort of chased me here." She drew a long shuddering breath. "But I'm still afraid. What if Koruz comes here and finds me? He will kill all of you just as he did my father. Did I do right to come here Grandfather?"

A soft smile spread across Grandfather's lined and tear-streaked face as he listened to this breathless explanation.

"You did right," he said, pulling her close to him. Noah looked quickly at Evalith who was standing with him at the foot of the raised sleeping platform that formed the bed. There was silent wonder in their faces at this sudden return of speech but Grandfather was so taken up with seeing Miriam that he did not even seem to notice.

"You must tell me where you have been. I have not ceased to pray for you but I was so worried, may God forgive me. God has been so good to bring you to my side once more! We must thank God for His goodness and mercy. We all deserve only death but in His mercy and love, He has been gracious."

These last words came only as a whisper as his face seemed to break into a thousand pieces. Only the uneven breathing of unfinished grief could be heard for some minutes. Then drawing a long unsteady breath, Methuselah whispered, "Noah, can you lead us in the hymn? You know the one I mean."

In hushed and shaky voices, the old melody from the beginning of time filled the tiny room. With the sound came a warm healing flow of peace to each heart and in the silence that followed, they could sense a presence as though God, Himself had joined them as they sang.

It was Noah who broke the stillness at last. "Most Holy and Almighty God, we humbly offer to You our sacrifice of praise. We praise You that You have come to us. Even though we deserve Your judgment, yet You have given us Your mercy. Even though we deserve to be forsaken, yet You have presenced Yourself with us this night. We worship you.

"Thank You for protecting Miriam and bringing her to us. We are all in Your hands. All around us men have turned from You and gone their own way. Even the thoughts of their hearts are evil continually. Only You can preserve our lives. Our eyes are upon You. Be pleased to keep your servants safe this whole night through and guide our steps in the new day as it comes."

In the stillness that followed this quiet prayer, footsteps could be heard moving stealthily along the back of the house. Miriam looked in terror at her uncle's face but he only waited quietly with his eyes on the door. Miriam could just make out the faint sound of the outer door and then the curtain of the doorway was pushed aside and Shem stepped inside.

"No one around, Father," he said quietly. "Ham is still watching, just in case, but I'm sure there was no one near enough to hear anything."

"Thank you Lord," murmured Noah.

"Now it is very late, but we cannot sleep until we are sure our guest has eaten. Shem, go and ask Deborah to bring some of the barley cakes and a little sweet wine. This is a time for celebration!" Evalith said briskly.

"Oh Auntie, I have had plenty to eat. The ark is fairly bulging with food," Miriam protested.

"We will eat a thank offering before the Lord then," put in Noah. "God has been so kind!"

Grandfather nodded his approval of this plan and shortly Deborah pushed her way into the room with a tray of small barley cakes flavored with honey and small cups of sweet fresh grape juice.

"Let me help you, Grandfather," Miriam said as Evalith started to kneel beside her.

The tray was placed on the floor and all sat on the goat-skin mats that covered the hard-packed earth. As they tasted the bread and wine, Miriam helped Grandfather and then took a bite or two and a sip of the wine. So great was her excitement that she could eat no more, but carefully rolled the cake in the flat leaf on which it rested and tucked it into her sleeve. It was a meal of joy eaten before the Lord God who had provided both the food and the occasion.

"Now all this excitement has worn Grandfather out. We must get to sleep," bustled Evalith. "Miriam, I have arranged a pallet here at the foot of Grandfather's bed. I was sure you would want to be near him. Tomorrow we will decide what to do next." She stepped to Miriam's side and drew her into a gentle embrace. "We are so thankful you are safe. We have prayed for you much these past days. Welcome to this house."

Miriam drew a shaky breath. "Oh Auntie, how can I thank you? I have been so alone these last weeks. I thought nothing could ever be right or safe again. I thought Grandfather was dead too." She wiped her streaming face with her sleeve. "I'm sorry. I don't seem to be able to do anything but cry."

"It's all right. Your cup of grief is very full. It will take some time for it to empty. But rest now and tomorrow will be easier."

The family moved quietly out of the room taking the tray with them and Miriam knelt once again beside Grandfather's low bed. For long minutes they simply clung to each other's hands and looked at each other. At last, Miriam spoke. "You were right, Grandfather. God did have another plan. I only wish I had trusted Him more. It would have been easier, I think."

"Where did you go? Where have you been all this time?"

"I hid in the field the first week and only came out at night. Then when I found you were gone, I decided to try to come to Uncle's house, like you told me but I only dared travel at night and I was afraid I would miss my way around the city. As it was, I met Koruz and one of his men right in the middle of the city somewhere but it was so dark that he didn't see me. After that I just went away from the direction I saw him go. But I heard him telling his men to find me so I knew I had to hide.

"I got so tired that I didn't think I could go another step and I prayed that God would guide me to a safe place to rest. Then that awful creature started to follow me and I just ran to get away from it. It chased me right into the ark. I didn't know where I was till yesterday."

As Miriam talked, Grandfather's eyes slowly closed and he let out a long sigh.

"Oh, Grandfather, you are tired, and here I am going on and on. Do you need a drink before you sleep? Here let me help you. There is still a little wine here in your cup."

Carefully, Miriam spooned a few mouthfuls between Grandfather's parched lips and he was able to swallow them with difficulty. Miriam was frightened at the change that she could see in his face. He was thinner and weaker than when she had last seen him. Yet his face seemed peaceful as he dropped into a light sleep.

Miriam changed into a fresh robe that Evalith had kindly left for her and lay down on the pallet at the foot of the bed and snuffed out the lamp. In the darkness, the steady sound of Grandfather's breathing comforted her.

"Thank you God. You have surely brought me here. I wish I had come sooner. Forgive me for doubting you. I hope I won't doubt you again. Help me to trust you like Uncle does."

In the silence that enveloped Noah's sturdy stone house, only the wind was awake and making conversation with the leaves of the trees. Listening to this gentle sound, Miriam was able to slowly relax and sink into a much-needed sleep.

Noah was first up, as usual, standing in the path inside the gate and looking through the dim pre-dawn light at the towering black form before him. It was really finished! This thought still surprised him somehow. He had been working toward this end for many, many years. His time rope that lay coiled in the remembrance box would show exactly how many years it had been.

"My Lord, what now? Is it time to move the family into the ark? Is this the day? Surely You have sent Miriam to us. Is she really the one? Make it plain Lord. I only want Your will to be done. Thank You for restoring Grandfather's speech. It will be a comfort to talk with him about all of these things. Poor Lomar, struck down so cruelly. And his sons will not come into the ark with us. Oh Lord, how can it be that their hearts are so hard? All the rest of my family, Lord! All gone away into their own ways, caring nothing for You or what You want. Can it really be that I am the only one?

"Dear Lord, I have given them Your message over and over and they only laugh and call me foolish or demented or worse! Can You not turn their hearts even now? See all the people of this great city. They will die. The babies, the old people, the children. Do they all have to die? Have mercy even yet, Lord. Have mercy!

"Yes, I know, You have been very patient. It must be almost one hundred years now that You have been patiently waiting, giving them time to repent, yet they only have grown worse and worse. Yes Lord, I see this is true. Each year they

104

are more evil. Yet my heart is heavy, full of anger at their stubbornness and yet also full of sorrow. How awesome that You are sharing Your sorrow with me! I lay my hand upon my mouth. Your sorrow is so much greater than I can imagine! You know each one! All their potential! All that You planned for them! Do You also feel this burning anger that they have turned their backs on such love and mercy? Today I will go again to the market place. I will speak again to all who will listen. Perhaps just one will turn back to You today."

Noah heard a step behind him and turned to see Shem beginning to fill the stone jar from the big cistern that sat beside the house.

"I'll just carry a few loads of water to the ark this morning. I'm sure the cattle will have finished all that we left them yesterday."

"There is more hay to be carried in as well. I'll send Ham and Japheth out to help you."

"Shall we move the family in today, do you think?"

"No, God has not yet said to move. He will tell us when the day arrives."

Ham's usually smiling face appeared at the door just then looking very sleepy.

"Ham, you had a long night. No sign of any spies about?"

"No, only more animals moving into the ark. Such a procession of scurrying and rustling! But no humans that I could detect, unless they had very small feet," answered Ham with his good-natured grin.

"I told Shem that I would send you along with a load of hay. Those animals will be hungry this morning."

"Me too!" Ham said. "This night business has my stomach growling like those black bears."

"All in good time, my empty cistern of a son. Your wife will have your food ready by the time you get finished," Noah answered as he started into the house.

Evalith, Loma and Deborah were hurrying around, preparing the morning meal. Loma coaxed the fire into life on the wide flat stone in the corner of the room. Above this stone were drying racks, smoked black with years of cooking and at the back were slats to keep hungry animals from the clay pots that sat in the embers.

This morning the freshly harvested grain was already ground and mixed with olive oil. Loma's delicate, but competent fingers shaped the mixture into small cakes and set them next to the fire where they would cook slowly.

As Noah sat in his favorite seat near the low table, Miriam stepped shyly from Grandfather's little room and moved toward the fire. She looked around the room fearfully as she came.

"God's morning to you, my child," Noah said. "What a miracle to see you here this morning. You remember Deborah and Loma. But then it has been a long time now. Perhaps Loma was not with us the last time we saw you. She is the wife of Ham, lucky fellow that he is."

"Where are your servants? When I was last here, you had many servants, Uncle."

Noah's happy smile died at this question and Miriam felt that she had very rude and forward to ask such a thing.

"Forgive me Uncle, I should not have asked. But that was one of the reasons that I was afraid to come here, because of the servants and how they would talk."

"No, No. It's all right to ask, little one. But it saddens me to think of them all gone. Some were drawn away by money, others driven away by threats and some who wanted to stay were struck down just as your father was." Noah sighed. "It is a wicked world, Miriam. God will judge them soon enough."

"The water is hot now, Miriam, if you want to take some to Grandfather," Evalith said, hoping to coax back a happier mood. For Evalith, all problems were best solved by doing something. It was the only way she had survived these years with her husband. If she kept busy enough, there was less time to think or worry or complain.

"Thank you Auntie. I'll take it to him," answered Miriam, glad to get on a different subject.

She took the warm stone water pot and the gourd dipper and carried them carefully to Grandfather.

"She is a good girl, Noah," Evalith said with a sigh. "She has willing hands and a gentle way about her. But how can we keep her hidden from Koruz? You know that he will find her sooner or later."

"Yes, I know. I know. But she has come to us and we cannot turn her away. She can help you with Grandfather. And as for Koruz, he is a God-sized problem and we will have to let God take care of it.

"In the meantime, I must talk with Japheth. I think God has brought us the wife of His choosing. I hope Japheth will be happy with His choice."

"Now don't rush them, Noah," said Evalith sitting for a moment on the bench near him. "Give them time to get acquainted a little before you bring it up. Miriam has been through so much grief, losing her father. She needs time to get used to the idea and to grieve properly for him."

"I know. It is not our custom to plan a marriage in the year of death. But God's commands are urgent and any day now we must move our family into the ark. I'm afraid we will not be able to plan a wedding for them. It would be too public and Koruz will not honor the fact that she has been given to another man."

"No wedding! That hardly seems right does it? Still..." she paused and drew her work worn hands across her eyes, "I don't know who would come if we had a wedding. Our former friends would be afraid to come and our enemies would only come to destroy." Evalith lifted her hands in despair.

107

"Ham is always saying that Japheth likes animals more than people. Maybe we will just invite that crowd out there in the ark. At least we could be sure that they would come."

"You can't be serious, Noah!" Evalith began indignantly but seeing the laughter in her husband's eyes she got up abruptly. "How can you make jokes at a time like this?" she asked with exasperation showing in her voice.

"It is just at such a time as this that we most need laughter, my dear. You know what I always say. Laughter is audible faith."

"Yes, I know," Evalith replied with a tired smile. "But it is more difficult to do than to say. And remember what your father used to say. 'A cheerful greeting too early in the morning is like a curse.'"

Noah chuckled and Evalith turned back to the washing of the fresh plums for breakfast with a small smile.

Miriam was glad for the excuse of helping Grandfather with his breakfast rather than joining the rest of her new family around the low table in the main room. She felt shy and a little confused, especially with the four men of the house. She needed time with Grandfather as well, to help her sort through all her feelings and share her grief with one who was there when her father was killed.

As she carried the tray into his room, his eyes met hers with a glad welcome. "I was hoping that you were really here and not just something that I had dreamed," Grandfather greeted her.

"Yes, I'm really here and I'm just as glad to know that you are truly here as well. I was so sure that you had been killed too, Grandfather. Now I just don't quite know where to put all the things I feel. I'm glad, sad, scared and angry all at the same time. Anyway," she said trying to smile, "if you eat a good breakfast, then I can know that you are really alive and hungry."

Grandfather smiled a rather lopsided smile but shook his head ever so slightly.

"Food doesn't really have much taste, Miriam."

"I've sweetened the porridge with lots of honey just the way you like it. Here. Try a bite."

With infinite care, Miriam slowly spooned the warm cereal into his mouth and even though she smiled encouragingly, she was dismayed at how little he was able to swallow. She found her own mouth opening with each bite she offered him and closed her mouth self-consciously.

"I'm trying to help you swallow each bite, Grandfather. Did you see how I was opening my mouth?" she asked, reaching for the cup to give him a sip of warm water.

"Just you being here is a help Miriam. You look so much like my wife, Hannah. She had golden hair like yours. Did I ever tell you that?"

"Yes, many times. Grandfather. I feel honored to look like her. Here, have a bit more porridge."

At last, Miriam sat back. He had emptied a small cup as well as all the warm water that she had brought. He seemed tired out from the effort and she quietly adjusted his pillow just the way he liked it. Then taking the tray she returned to the kitchen.

The men had all gone out and she carried the tray to the table. Evalith was there stemming raisins.

"Sit down now, Miriam. I know how tedious it is to help him eat but you've done well. I haven't been able to get him to take that much food since he came."

"He likes his porridge with lots of honey," Miriam said smiling in spite of herself. "But he is so weak. He wasn't like this when I last saw him. Will he regain his strength?"

"It's very hard to tell. Yesterday he ate less and was not able to talk. Today he can do both. We will just have to take it a day at a time."

Miriam sat across from Evalith and began pulling the plump raisins from the stem. She nibbled one or two as she worked. Her mind was full of so many uncertainties that it was comforting just to take up this mindless task. Deborah and Loma had gone for water and the house was quiet around them. At last, after a heavy sigh, Miriam spoke.

"Have you heard any news from my mother or sister? Japheth said my brother has been here. I just wondered if he said anything about them."

"He didn't mention them. We just assumed that they are still there at your home."

"Oh no, they are gone! Grandfather told me that Koruz took them both to his house the day he killed my father."

"Oh my dear! We didn't know that! Grandfather hasn't been able to tell us anything and we don't spend any time at the market where we would hear about it. Oh I am so sorry!"

Evalith put down the raisins and wiping her hands on her hand cloth, she came and put her arm around Miriam.

"I told Noah you had lost your father and needed time to grieve but I didn't know the others were gone too. Surely he did not take your mother into his harem, did he?"

"Grandfather said he seemed to think she might have another blond child like me. He doesn't know it came from my father's side. Oh why did I have to have this silly colored hair? All the trouble started because of it. If God had only given me lovely dark hair like Deborah."

"Now child, Noah's father used to say, 'God must like variety. He makes people in all shapes and sizes and colors.' Noah says that we must trust Him. He knows best even when we can't understand."

"Yes, Grandfather has always taught me that too."

Miriam glanced around the large central room that served the home in so many ways. Wool was lying in a great heap at one side, waiting to be spun into thread. Cakes of raisins lay on the shelf on large flat banana leaves, waiting to be carried to the ark. A big pile of almonds lay on a mat, each one gaping open like a clam, waiting to have the delicious nuts removed and stored when they were dry enough.

The stillness and peace of the room was like a balm to Miriam. Her eyes became bright with unshed tears as she spoke again. "I thought my life was over when Father betrothed me to Laban. He does not believe in God at all any more and he works for Koruz. But Grandfather said we would just pray and ask God for His best. And then Koruz saw me at the betrothal dinner. Auntie, he tried to buy me right there at the dinner, in front of all our guests. When Father said 'no' he seemed to accept it. But then he told Laban he would kill him if he married me so Laban came back and broke the engagement. I was out of one problem and into a worse one. And now I'm here and if Koruz finds me, he may kill all of you just to get me.

"I should never have come here. I bring only trouble to you. I must go far away somewhere where no one will know me." Miriam's words ended in a sob and the tears of many days overflowed again.

"Now, now, you mustn't talk like that. Remember how God has protected you and brought you here. Surely you must not despise His goodness and care. And Grandfather needs you. I think his improvement today is because of his joy in seeing you. He needs you and I need you too."

"I know, Auntie, but I am still so afraid..."

Her words were cut short by the two women returning from the well with their water. They set down the heavy clay jars and rushed into the room.

"The river has stopped!" Loma burst out. "You know the big river that Koruz was going to bring into the city. The girls at the well were all talking about it and they said it is only a trickle now."

"They said the rocky hill above it just collapsed and hardly any water is in the river now," Deborah put in.

"It must have happened yesterday when everything shook," Loma said excitedly. "Koruz is hiring all the men he can find to go and try to clear away the rocks and dirt."

"Have you told the men yet? They will want to know because of the herds that are there," Evalith said, a worried frown deepening the lines between her eyes.

"I'll go," Loma said and was out the door before another word could be said.

"Father will hear it too," said Deborah as she gathered up the clothing she was planning to wash. "He went to the market to preach this morning when we left for the water."

"I hope he gets home safely. Lately the people seem to get so angry at his preaching. It used to be that they would only laugh but now the whole mood has changed. If anything bad happens, their first thought is to somehow blame Noah. They will probably find some way to blame the earthquake on him.

"Why can't they see that it is their own sin that is bringing God's judgment on them?" Evalith got up and went out to the gate to see if she could see Noah returning.

The path leading to the market was empty but she could hear people shouting and whistling. There seemed to be a large crowd and the noise was coming closer. Her fears grew when Noah broke into view, walking swiftly and close behind was a shouting, screaming mob, throwing stones and pieces of wood. She could see blood streaming down the side of his face and she started to open the gate to run to him. Then she thought of Miriam. Turning quickly she hurried into the house.

"Quickly Miriam, come out back of the house. We have a big pile of flax drying there and you can hide under it. Quickly! There is a big crowd following Noah home and they are very angry."

Miriam darted out the door and Deborah who was there washing helped cover her completely with the drying flax. Then she went back to her washing, saying quietly, "I'm right here Miriam. I will distract them if they come back here."

Evalith hurried back through the house and met Noah as he came in the gate. The crowd was close behind him, still shouting and throwing stones and dirt.

"Go in the house, Evalith! You might get hit," Noah gasped.

"But you are hurt already. Surely they will not harm me. You go on in the house."

The crowd had stopped outside the wall that ringed the compound, and Noah turned to face them.

"My friends, I beg of you. Do not demean yourselves in this way. You are made in the image of God. He has planned a long and fruitful life for you if only you will walk in His way. Turn your anger against the evil one and the evil in your midst, not against me for pointing to the evil. God will still have mercy. Think what our father Adam would say to us. Think what your ancestor Seth would say. Remember the words of Enoch who walked these very streets and taught us what God wanted us to be. We are to love one another, not hate."

"Don't talk to us about love," shouted one of the sellers from the market. "We know what kind of love we want and we will get it too."

"Keep your sermons to yourself from now on," shouted another, punctuating his words with curses "or we will do more than throw stones. And leave our river alone!"

"I quite approve your plan for wise use of the river, but you must remember it is God's river. And we are all under His command to make good use of it for the good of all the people," Noah countered.

This agreement brought looks of surprise to many faces and there was a murmur that rippled through the crowd. One of Koruz's men felt the change and quickly stepped forward.

"We know you did something to stop that river," he shouted. "We saw you and your boys running in from that valley yesterday. Koruz will see that you don't get any of the water when we get the river open and running again. We won't forget all the work you've caused us."

Noah started to speak, but Evalith laid a hand on his arm and quietly turned him toward the house. A few stones followed them but the crowd began to turn away and no one dared to come through the gate uninvited.

Chapter Nine

It was a gloomy group who gathered around the evening meal. Evalith's mouth was set in a grim line as she placed the food on the table. Noah appeared withdrawn and preoccupied as he blessed the food. Deborah and Loma nervously toyed with their food and started up at any small noise from outside. Shem and Ham ate in grim silence, their faces showing the weariness of the long tense day.

It was Shem who had told the story in his terse, organized way. "We rode out to the pasture where the herds had been. The river is now only a tiny trickle. The herds are gone. A few remain, maybe fifteen or twenty. The rock face above the river looked as though it had exploded outward. Now there is just a jumble of boulders and stones.

"We could only stand and stare. How merciful that we started back with the cattle when we did. House-sized rocks have bounced and rolled across the plain and almost certainly most of the herds of cattle and sheep are now buried under the rubble.

"Koruz was there with a large crowd of his men. He was studying the scene with an angry face and his men were casting dark looks in the our direction.

"Koruz came over, but before he even reached us he started shouting. He didn't give a greeting or anything. Just bellowed, 'What have you done to the river?'

"'It is not in man's power to do this. Surely you know that,' I said. 'The earth itself moved yesterday. No doubt this rock face was broken at that time. We were there early in the day,' and I pointed to the great slope of broken stones, 'and all was quiet. We started a few of our cattle back towards home and were about half way there when we felt and heard the earth move. Our animals broke and ran, arriving at the ark about the time your men were there searching the ark. You can ask them. They saw us there.'

"But I think he knew that and was just bellowing for the benefit of the people there. He said, 'You don't care about anyone but yourself. You don't care that this river was to flow through our city and bring its life into reach of everyone there. You will have to help the rest of the town's people to clear the river. We must roll away and clear the debris until the water is free to flow again. I will expect to see you here tomorrow when we begin.'"

"He really expects us to be there tomorrow," put in Ham. "He'll look for us and if we aren't there, he'll come here, or send his men to find out why."

Noah nodded acknowledgment but Japheth's mind was still with the flock.

"Why?" he exploded, looking at his father. "Why would God shake the mountain and deliberately kill all our flocks? Surely those innocent animals have done Him no wrong! I just don't see any sense in this." He got up abruptly and paced around the room.

"Japheth, we can't really ask 'why' questions of God and expect Him to account to us. We owe our very existence to Him. The breath of our mouth is from Him. He made those animals. They are His to do with as He chooses." Noah's voice was patient but all could hear the deep sadness in it.

"I can't help it. I just can't see why He allows all this pain. If He really loves us, wouldn't He protect our animals? It just doesn't seem right that they suffer for man's sin!"

Evalith put out a hand to stop him as he swung past her.

"My son, God is not to blame for your pain or theirs. You know that, I'm sure."

He stared down at her for a moment, his eyes dark with anger and bitter questions.

"Japheth," Noah's voice was tired but gentle, "Your anger and grief is not just for your precious animals, my son. That is only the most recent hurt. No doubt your heart is still thinking about Rhoda. I wish too that God would explain all the reasons for pain but probably if He did, we still wouldn't understand. But we can still trust Him to do what is best."

Japheth thrust a impatient hand through his dark unruly hair and pulled away from his mother's hand and continued his pacing.

"His ways are not our ways. But it is we who are foolish and not God. I feel your pain too, but not just for our herds, and not just for Rhoda. Do you not realize that all the animals and all the people will soon be destroyed! God has said that He will flood the earth with water. Only those who are in the ark will survive. Think of that pain!" Noah drew a long breath and buried his face in his hands for several long silent moments. His voice was barely audible as he continued, "God takes no pleasure in the death of the wicked. But man's wickedness has grown monstrous. They think only of evil continually. They love no one but themselves. They refuse to love God or even keep Him in their memory anymore. They are full of anger, hatred, pride, lust and every evil thing." Noah's face crumpled and tears poured down the deep lines of his face.

"I have tried all my life to make them see," he went on, "but not one will listen... not one! My very own brothers and sisters! All my boyhood friends! All my servants! All my uncles and aunts who are the brothers and sisters of my father! No one will listen to God any more. All they want is their own way. They heard the truth from Methuselah, they heard it from my father, and they have heard it from me but no! No one cares. They just go on becoming more wicked each day! They are so wicked that they don't even know what wickedness is any more. They call me wicked for warning them." Noah's shoulders shook with pain too deep for any sound.

Silence filled the room as even Japheth stopped pacing. Shem started to say something but before he could form his thoughts into words, there was a whisper of movement from the doorway and Miriam who had been standing there listening, came slowly to Noah's side. Kneeling beside him, she reached out and touched his hand. "I will listen, Uncle. I want to hear all that God has said. There is so much that I don't understand. But I have found in these past days that God does still care. Please don't give up now."

Noah took her small but capable hand in his big gnarled one. The pitch from the ark still stood out black beneath his nails. The years of handling timbers had left great calluses across his palms. His breath came in long quivering gasps but his eyes were tender as he looked down into Miriam's pale face.

"Miriam," He said at last, pausing to brush away the tears with the back of his hand. "Miriam, you are God's gift to me today. He has sent you to me to remind me of my dear sons and their wives and of my faithful Evalith. You are right. God forgive me. I must never again say that no one listens."

At that moment, some animal with hard hooves could be heard moving past the house in the direction of the ark and Noah smiled, "Even the animals have listened! Just hear those two hurrying to get in the door. Japheth, they are wiser than the people, aren't they. And never forget that God has made provision for them to live too. Just look at the size of that ark!

"Our herds will live on in the offspring of those that we brought in yesterday. Come, we must praise Him for this." And he began the ancient song of praise and one by one the others joined him. And from the bedroom came a wavering voice singing the last line after they had all finished. Grandfather may have been a little late, but he could once again offer his sacrifice of praise and he intended to do it.

As Miriam slipped away to see if Grandfather needed anything, she heard Shem say, "But what about our immediate problem? Shall we go out and help clear away the stones from the river?"

"Yes, you and Ham must go, even though it is a futile effort and perhaps dangerous. Japheth and I will stay here and continue to carry in provisions. I feel we must move into the ark very soon and all must be ready. God is holding back His judgment, waiting for His perfect time. He has not shown me when this will be but I will know, I'm sure. God never gets in a hurry because He always starts in time."

The women rose to clear away the remains of the meal as Miriam moved to Grandfather's bedside. Grandfather was still awake as Miriam entered and he held up his hand and took hers. Tears crept unbidden down his cheeks but his eyes were bright with joy.

"Miriam, remember our talk a few weeks ago when you said there was no right decision for you and there was no hope. God is now showing us that He did have another plan for you. Not Laban. Not Koruz. But the one man who needs you and has not sold himself to Koruz. Your cousin Japheth. He needs you. Shall I speak to his father for you? God has put this responsibility into my hands now because you own father is dead."

Miriam knelt beside the low bed, keeping her voice very low.

"But it is not seemly to speak of a wedding so soon after Father's death. How can I answer such a question now?" Her voice cracked and she covered her face with her hands.

"Miriam, there can be no wedding, in the manner of this city. There can be no guests outside this family. It is not safe. And my time may be short. This is one thing I must do before I sleep with my fathers.

"I must ask again, would you accept Japheth as your husband? I believe it is for your good and God is leading, but still I will not force any union on you." Grandfather's whispery voice carried such loving concern that Miriam could not speak for several minutes. Then she lifted her eyes to his and nodded slowly.

"I would accept him, if he asks, Grandfather. And if Uncle Noah agrees that it is all right. Maybe next year things will be different and we can marry then. If Koruz doesn't find me first."

"No, we can not wait a year. I will speak to Noah now. Please ask him to come to me."

Miriam rose quietly, a blush tingeing her fair skin with an attractive glow, she went into the main room and told Noah that Grandfather was calling for him.

"I was just coming to see him," said Noah. "Please, Miriam, stir the fire a bit and heat us some milk with a bit of honey and spice. We will have a quiet cup together after this difficult day."

Noah entered the dim bedroom and sat on the cushion beside the bed. The single lamp threw flickering shadows on his face as he looked down at his now frail ancestor. He could still remember him in his prime, a strong vibrant man who towered over him and exuded boundless energy. He was startled by the thought that when he first remembered him, he would have been about the age he himself was now. Could it really have been more than five hundred years ago? It was his unshakable love for God that had kindled his own heart to know this Creator. What a lot he owed to this man.

"Grandfather, you wanted to see me? Miriam will bring us a little refreshment in a moment and we can treasure a little time together."

"It is good. We have had little of that these last years. I was just thinking of when you were born. What a talker you were in your early years. You were so filled with words that they just seemed to overflow as though you had a huge supply to use and too little time to use them."

Methuselah smiled at the memory and Noah's eyes twinkled. "I must have inherited that from you. But as you, I have learned to listen more than I speak. I got that from you, too. You said your father Enoch taught you that it was much more important to hear God's thoughts than to express your own. I have found that to be so very true."

Miriam brought the tray then and held the cup while Grandfather had a sip or two of the warm, sweet liquid. He smiled at her and then dismissed her with a nod.

"Noah, it is good to remember all that God has done, but I feel that there is still one thing that I must do." His chin trembled at the effort to speak so much but he continued. "Miriam was betrothed to Laban, but before the wedding could be planned, Koruz demanded her. You know the terrible results of that. But now I feel that Miriam is my responsibility. Her brothers have sworn to give her to Koruz. She has cared for me so many years and she has confided in me her fears and hopes. She was very sad when her father betrothed her to Laban because he did not love our Creator. How much more she dreaded the thought of belonging to the godless Koruz! She asked me if there was no one in all the world who still loved and honored God.

"After her father was killed, we had only one brief talk and we agreed together to ask God for His solution. I believe He has answered, though I would never have chosen His way."

"Nor I, Grandfather. Still I can see that He was answering my prayer as well, in bringing her to me. My only regret is that I did not think of her sooner. I heard that she was betrothed to Laban and gave it no more thought. If only I had known her heart then, I would have come to her father months ago. But I have been so busy getting everything finished here that I just didn't listen properly. I am sorry to have been so careless that I forced God to work in a more drastic way than He would wish. Forgive my busyness LORD."

"God's ways are higher than our ways, my son. He knows your heart and remembers that you are only dust. He forgives."

Both men were silent for many minutes and then Methuselah reached a shaky hand for the cup, lifted it to Noah's and said, "If you wish Miriam for your son, Japheth, she is willing."

"I wish it with all my heart," replied Noah and they each sipped their drink, although Noah had to help Grandfather a bit.

"How can it be arranged under the present circumstances and when?" asked Noah. "No one must know in the city, or Koruz will be here to drag her away."

"Yes, I have been thinking of that. But I remember when I was only a young man that there was no big feast or wedding as is the custom now. It was a simple agreement between families with a celebration dinner. Let us call back the old way for Miriam and Japheth. These modern ways are only an exercise of pride and self-importance. Let us simply ask God to join them as He did our father Adam and his wife Eve. Let's acknowledge that He has done this and not we ourselves."

"It is good," Noah replied breathing a long sigh of relief that this problem at least had a solution.

Chapter Ten

It was a quiet wedding. None of the usual decorations or fine clothes. None of the endless cooking and preparations that always marked weeklong wedding feasts. The men had gone about their work that day as though it were just any other day, with Shem and Ham spending the time struggling with the broken rocks at the riverbed and Noah and Japheth making endless trips to carry more provisions into the ark. Only the women scurried about making special sweet cakes and gathering all the fruits that were available.

"I wish we could go to the market for some flowers," Evalith said as evening approached. "They would make the table look festive."

"If I could go home, we could have plenty of orange blossoms," said Miriam. "Father's grove is always in bloom."

"There are jasmine bushes near the city well," Loma offered.

"People might wonder why you wanted them," Evalith objected. "We don't want anyone to start any talk. We'll just have to make do with what we have."

"How I wish I had my clothes from home," Miriam sighed. "Mother made me a beautiful pale green dress for the betrothal dinner. She spent so many hours on it. If only she could be with us today. It doesn't seem like a wedding day without family and friends." She sighed again.

Evalith came and put her arm around her shoulder. "I know how you must feel. You have had no time to even think these past days to say nothing of planning to be married. We live in a very difficult time. Nothing is right any more." She sighed and shook her head suddenly as if to shake away the thoughts that were pressing in on her.

"We will just have to praise God for what we have and forget about those things we don't have. You miss your father and mother, I know. I miss all my friends and family too. Once this house would have been full for a day like this. But now, even if we invited them, they would not come." There was a tinge of bitterness in her voice. "They would make up good excuses. They would say how much they wish they could be here. But they would not come, even if we dared to invite them and even for the food they would not come!"

"My family couldn't attend my wedding either," put in Loma who was tending cakes on the hearth, "but I wasn't sorry! They would have made the day a misery for me. They only knew how to be cruel and never kind. Only Mother would have rejoiced for me, if she had still been alive."

"God is not limited by our traditions," said Evalith. "He can always do a new thing or bring us back to an old way as we're doing today, and we must accept that He knows what He is doing. When I was married, no one ever thought of having a wedding so soon after the death of a parent. It just wasn't done."

"I would wait too, Auntie, if Uncle and Grandfather would allow it but they both agree that it must be now. Can it really be that God will soon judge all the people in a great flood? Grandfather always said that God loves us and cares for us. I can't imagine that He will destroy everyone."

Evalith's face grew grim. "Child, you have not known all the evil that is around us; all the people who have been killed like your father and the dear girl that was betrothed to Japheth. If God is a just God, surely He must judge such evil. He can not let it go on and on."

"But He has let it go on and on!" put in Loma. "Nothing ever happens to them. They just go on and on eating, drinking, marrying and going to someone else's wedding."

"My husband says that God has been waiting for the ark to be finished and giving men more time to repent. If he is wrong then these past one hundred years have been totally wasted—building and building; preaching and preaching. No one listens. They only laugh or throw stones. And now they have turned so hostile that each day I pray they will not kill him too." Evalith's eyes reddened with unshed tears but her hands worked faster and faster.

"The women at the well this morning were talking about the river being stopped up and they were looking at me as though I was somehow to blame," said Deborah. "Mahazia who used to help in the vineyard came edging up to me and whispered that the men were talking about burning the ark. He said that we should be ready to run away if we wanted to live. I couldn't tell if he was trying to be kind or trying to make us afraid."

"If it was the latter, he surely succeeded," said Loma grimly. "What if we move into the ark and then they set it on fire? What can we do then except run like rats?"

"Now girls, Father says that God has commanded the ark as a place of safety and He will protect it. If we can't trust Him for that, then we have nothing at all to trust in." Evalith turned her kindest smile on Miriam. "Come. Let's get the new bedding into the wedding chamber that was so recently a storeroom. We'll all feel better if we keep busy."

Later, when the men were returning, Miriam laid a trembling hand on Evalith's arm. "Do you think we could carry Grandfather out here to the main room, so that he could be with us? Would it be too much for him?"

"What a good idea! I'm sure we can arrange to make him comfortable here on this side of the table. Let's move things so there will be room beside you, Miriam. The boys can carry him out when they get here."

"I'll go tell Grandfather," Miriam said as she disappeared through the curtain to his room.

He seemed to be asleep when Miriam entered but when she began straightening the bedding and pouring fresh water into his cup, he opened his eyes and smiled.

"I didn't mean to waken you, Grandfather, but your blanket was all twisted and it looked so uncomfortable."

"I was not really asleep. I was listening to the comfortable bustle going on in the other room. I can even smell the sweet cakes baking on the hearth." His face crumpled into tears for several minutes as so often happens when one has had a stroke. At last he gained control and continued. "This is a special day for you Miriam, but it has come upon you so suddenly that you may feel frightened. Come, sit beside me and tell me what you are thinking." He reached his bony hand up and Miriam took it as she sat down.

Grandfather studied her face for several minutes and then sighed. Miriam did not meet his gaze as this would have been too bold, but she did acknowledge his look with a glance before staring resolutely at her hands.

"You begin a journey into a new life today, Miriam. You have not been there before and we all fear the unfamiliar. But our God has always planned for our good and I feel very sure that He has planned this marriage for you and for Japheth. When it is so dark ahead, I feel comforted that you will have the protection of a man who still acknowledges God."

126

"I still don't feel safe, Grandfather." Her voice was little more than a whisper. "I still feel that Koruz will burst in and carry me away. Or my brother will come and find me here and take me to him. I can't seem to let my heart rest even after all that God has done."

"But what about your marriage? Do you have any joy at the prospect?"

"Japheth was kind to me when he found me in the ark. But I haven't had time to think about what it will be to be his wife. I still want to be here for you when you call. I just don't quite know what to do about that."

"Talk to Evalith about it. She can advise you about those things. And you are not going to another place. This is the home of your husband. Isn't God kind to plan even this small detail for you?"

"I guess so," Miriam said softly, "but so much has happened that I can't really seem to think. I am just going along in what seems like a dream. I hope I don't wake up but I'm not sure I'm safe even in my dream."

Methuselah sighed. He closed his eyes for a bit and then began almost to himself.

"It was one of the things that was more damaged by our sin than any other... this natural trust in our God. When Grandfather Adam sinned, the first thing that entered his heart was fear! Great fear! He said they had never felt such a thing before: fear and shame. Many times I have seen him cry and tell how wonderful it was when there was no fear, only love. But sin brought fear, like a creeping disease and it has spread through all of us. Only now, men don't fear God any more. They only fear other men. It is a sad day."

Miriam sat quietly for a time and then suddenly started! "Grandfather, I almost forget to tell you why I came in. We are planning to bring you to our table tonight so we can all be together. I must help you get a clean robe on and smooth your hair and beard. You can help us celebrate tonight."

127

The tears started again. "That is good, Miriam. I will enjoy the change of scenery," he whispered.

So it was that Grandfather was stretched out beside the low table that night, propped up on pillows and honored with the first serving of each festive dish that was provided. Miriam and Japheth sat next to him with Noah and his wife on the other side. Shem and Ham and their wives completed the wedding party.

The table was spread with sweet smelling leaves and the foods were piled in rich abundance, baked tubers, bean porridge, fruits, honey cakes and fresh grape juice, sweetened with honey and heated over the fire.

Noah led the family in their traditional song of thanksgiving and invited the Lord God to bless this gathering with His own dear presence as He had when He brought Eve to Adam. Methusalah recounted in halting words the story of that first wedding which he had heard from Adam's own lips.

"It was more than sixteen hundred years ago now, when God arranged that first wedding. Adam had finished naming all the animals and as he walked with the Lord God that night, he confided that somehow he still felt lonely. All the animals had their mates but he had none. God assured him that He had a plan to fill that need, and when next he awoke, there was Eve in all her beauty. God, Himself gave them to each other and it was a time of great joy.

"It is with the very words from Adam himself, spoken at the beginning of time in the presence of the Lord God that we join Japheth and Miriam tonight. Let us say them together.

"And Adam said, 'This is now bone of my bone and flesh of my flesh: she shall be called Woman because she was taken out of Man. Therefore shall a man leave his father and his mother and shall cleave unto his wife: and they shall be one flesh.'"

Methuselah stretched out his shaky hands and laid one on Miriam's head and the other on Japheth's bowed head. "What God has joined together, let no man put asunder."

Then in quavering tones he began the ancient hymn of praise and all joined in softly, ever mindful of those who might be listening outside.

Later, after Grandfather had been carefully carried back to his bed and Miriam had given a few unnecessary last minute instructions to the smiling Evalith, the newlyweds were ushered to the wedding chamber.

When they were alone, they looked at each other shyly. Japheth still could see the face of his beloved Rhoda in his mind. Miriam could not dismiss that awful sight of her father as he fell under Koruz's hand. But this mingled grief pulled them into each other's arms and there they were comforted.

Miriam was up early the next morning, wearing one of Loma's robes. She smiled down at the sleeping form of her husband, marveling at God's mercy. She must get the fire started and check on Grandfather to see if he needed anything. She started to pull back the curtain when she heard Noah speaking. She paused, wondering if they had visitors at such an early hour. She peeped cautiously around the edge of the curtain but could see no one there. It was still quite dark with only dim pre-dawn light filtering through the open door. Quietly she stepped out and approached the door to assure herself that there were none of Koruz's men there. Noah was standing by the gate, head bowed, listening to some voice she could not hear, but responding occasionally.

"Seven days, Lord God? Only seven days?" a long pause and then, "Yes Lord, we will begin today. Thank you for sending Miriam to us. Your timing is right I know but I can hardly face what is to come. Give us Your strength Lord God. Help us to do all that You have commanded."

Miriam moved to the hearth and began to stir the coals that were still burning there. As she added a bit of wood shavings, and blew on the fire, Noah came up behind her.

"You are up early, Miriam. It is good. We must wake the others. God has told me that in seven days the great judgment will begin and we must move into the ark at once."

Miriam glanced up at him and was startled to see how white his face had become.

"I'll waken Japheth," she said, "and see to Grandfather's needs as quickly as I can."

Noah went from room to room, stirring the whole household to a flurry of excitement. Evalith, practical as always, stopped them abruptly.

"Wait! There are seven days to do this. We must have breakfast before we begin. Come girls, let's get the food on the table as always. Then we can begin to move our necessary things after that. We can at least have one last quiet meal in this house." Her voice betrayed her calm manner when her throat constricted on that word 'house'. She turned away to get the cakes that were left from the night before.

"Here Miriam, let me do the fire while you take Grandfather his breakfast," said Deborah, hastily fastening up her hair beneath her head cloth.

"It's all right. He will want his warm water to drink anyway. You go ahead with the meal."

Each one fell to their early morning routine but their minds were racing. This day had been so long expected and yet now that it was here, they found themselves savoring each task as 'the last time I will do this here.'

Grandfather was awake when Miriam pushed into the small bedroom with the pitcher of warm water and the porridge he usually ate.

"Good morning, Grandfather! I see you are awake as usual. I hope you slept well."

"Miriam! You are a welcome sight. I was longing for a drink."

"Yes, I thought you might be. Let me wash away the sleep a little with this warm wet cloth, and then I will help you to sit up."

"You look much like your great grandmother, Miriam. Have I ever told you that your eyes are just like hers... and your hair."?

"Yes, Grandfather. Many times." She helped him sit up a bit and propped the pillows behind him.

"I will see her soon now," murmured Grandfather as he took the cup from Miriam's hand. "Very soon."

Miriam watched as he sipped his drink, struggling with each swallow and wondered if his mind was wandering.

Suddenly he glanced up at her, as if she had just come in. His eyes brightened in happy surprise and he started to rise, sliding his legs off the side of the cot with surprising strength and quickness.

"Hannah! You've come! How wonderful to see you." Miriam turned quickly to see if someone had come in behind her but there was no one there. Then, in slow motion, as a great tree beginning its seemingly endless fall, Grandfather fell forward off his bed, down through her arms and onto the floor.

"Grandfather!" shouted Miriam. "Japheth, help me! Grandfather has fallen!"

The family gathered quickly around the still   f o r m . Noah knelt down and turned him gently onto his back.

"Here Shem, help me lift him back onto the bed." With great care they laid him down and Noah bent a long time, listening for either breath or heart beat. There was neither.

"He's gone! GONE!" The word came out in a long wailing cry. Every face seemed to twist and crumple as the realization spread through their minds. Wails of grief came unbidden as they stared at his wasted form. Miriam could still

131

see on his face that look of incredulous delight. Through her tears, she gently touched his face and traced the smile lines there. "He looks so happy. He thought he saw Grandmother Hannah and he tried to get up to go to her. I've never seen him look so before."

Noah spread his arms around his sobbing family and their tears fell together as each felt the loss and loneliness that this death brought.

"I can't imagine life without him," Noah murmured. All my years, six hundred of them, he has been there. He was my encourager when God spoke to me about the coming judgment. His faith never wavered when all his sons except my father and Miriam's father turned away from God."

"I must inform the relatives of his death, Father," said Shem. "They will have heard our weeping and no doubt are even now gathering to discuss it."

"Miriam! This is a time of great danger for you," said Japheth. "Many will come to pay their respects and grieve with us. Come, I must take you to the ark, before it is fully light."

"Japheth is right," put in Evalith. "Why not cover yourself with one of Japheth's cloaks and go with him quickly. I will care for Grandfather. You have finished your task here and must be out of sight before anyone comes."

"Our move into the ark will have to wait a few days," said Noah. He was looking at Methuselah and did not see the look of relief that came over Evalith's face.

"Shem, as soon as Miriam is safe, go and tell those who must be told. I am not sure any will come to my house, even to honor their own patriarch, but they must be told. Evalith, you, Deborah and Loma will have to prepare food and drink for all who come. Hurry now, before someone is at the door."

In the midst of all the arrangements, Noah retired to his own bedroom and kneeling down, drew a small chest from its niche in the base of the wall. As he opened it, he felt the weight of years bear down on him. Here were the precious names, each listed on the clay tablets with their birth date, the birth of their first son, and the dates of their deaths. As he began his preparation for adding the day of Grandfather's death to the family history, he silently counted the knots on the time rope that recorded the years of Methuselah. It took a long time, as each year was marked with a knot on the long curling rope made from the hairs of Methuselah's own head. Nine hundred and sixty nine years! This living time line traced his life from the fine brown hair of youth, through the strong dark, almost black years of his strength and finally into the white more and more fragile hairs of age. He tied the final knot.

The last link was gone! Now there was no one alive who knew Adam and Eve—no remembrancer except himself. "Methuselah. His name means 'when he dies, it will come'." Cold realization spread over Noah. This was God's confirmation of the message he had heard that morning. God had said, "Come into the ark, you and all your household, because I have seen that you alone are righteous before Me in this generation. After seven more days I will cause it to rain on the earth forty days and forty nights and I will destroy from the face of the earth all living things that I have made."

"Seven more days! Seven days of mourning for Methuselah and mourning for all mankind."

Chapter Eleven

The morning mist was still heavy and close to the ground as Miriam and Japheth hurried toward the ark. They tried to walk casually but inward fear quickened each step until they were almost running by the time they reached the ramp. Miriam was about halfway up when a voice behind them froze them in mid-stride.

"Japheth! What is happening? My wife said she heard noises at your house this morning." It was Mar, a neighbor who lived across the fields.

Japheth glanced at Miriam who quickly moved on up the ramp and into the welcoming darkness. Japheth turned back.

"Mar, I didn't see you there. Is your family well?"

"Well, thank you. And yours?"

"It's a day of great sadness for this city. Grandfather Methuselah died early this morning. Shem is just going into town to make the report and the women sent me out to bring them some of the fresh grain for grinding. We will have preparations ready for visitors soon."

Japheth looked toward the house and was relieved to see Shem striding toward them.

"There is Shem now. He can walk back with you on his way to town and tell you all about it."

Mar looked up the ramp and then back at Japheth.

"I didn't see you at the river yesterday. Koruz asked me to remind you that he expects every able-bodied man to be there."

"My father and I had to take care of the animals here yesterday and surely he will understand that today we must prepare Grandfather for burial. Take him word that my family will be in mourning this week. Seven days are the least we can do for one so ancient and honored as Grandfather. I'm sure he will want to express his sorrow also."

"Koruz will not be pleased. You'd better have Shem take the message personally. I wouldn't want to be the one to bring him a message like that."

With a brief nod toward Shem, he glanced again at the ramp and then headed back toward his home.

"Trouble?" asked Shem as he approached.

"I don't know yet. I'm sure he saw Miriam as she went up ahead of me but I don't know if he suspected who it was. He said Koruz was angry that I was not in the work party yesterday and that you must take word to him yourself if you are not going out today."

"Did you tell him about Grandfather?"

"Yes. His wife must have been outside early and heard our cries. She sent him to see what had happened, not that they cared but it was a good excuse to come and have a look."

Japheth looked around carefully and then started up the ramp. "I'll make sure Miriam is safely hidden first and then I'll go with you if you want."

"No. You stay and help get the grave prepared. The ground is hard and the cave we always used was in the hillside above the river. There is no way we can go there or even find it since the earthquake."

"I hadn't thought of that." He stood still for a long moment, his mind struggling to take in all the sudden changes: his marriage, his father's message of only seven days till judgment,

Grandfather's death and now even uncertainty as to where he should be buried. He wiped his hand over his face. What would happen next? Shem laid a hand briefly on his shoulder and turned toward town. Japheth hurried into the ark.

As his eyes accustomed themselves to the darkness he moved toward the ladder. At the top, he looked down into the bin of straw where he had first seen his cousin a few days ago. Now she was his wife. Why did it seem so long ago?

"Miriam, are you there?" he called softly.

The straw moved in the corner below him and Miriam's head appeared.

"Yes, Japheth. I'm here," she whispered. "Has the man gone? Did he ask about me?"

"I think he saw you but he couldn't have known who you were in that cloak. It was a good thing Mother suggested it. Will you be all right there? Can I bring you anything?"

"No, I'm all right. But please Japheth, pray! I'm so scared. If that man suspects, then he will bring others to search again."

"Father says this ark is a place of safety planned and built on God's commands. You are safe here. Just don't try to go anywhere else. I couldn't bear to lose you too."

Their eyes locked for a long moment and then Japheth turned to the pile of new grain and scooped some into the leather pouch he had snatched up as they left the house.

"I'll be back when I can," called Japheth softly as he went down the ladder.

It was another endless day for Miriam as she listened intently for the sounds of a search that she hoped would not come. Warm feelings for Japheth brought blushes to her cheeks and fear for his safety constricted her throat. Then Grandfather's dear face swam into focus in her mind and the reality of his death broke open her well of tears again. The death wail started to rise unbidden in her throat but she stifled it before it could be heard. She could not even mourn him properly. He had been her constant care for more than thirty years and now she was not even permitted the release of the death hymn. "Oh God. I was born in an evil time. There is no good anywhere. There is no familiar custom left us. Are you really there? Are you really good? Dead! Grandfather is dead just like Father. But it was so different. He looked so happy! He looked young, like I remember him when I was a little girl. I will never forget that look. It is there in my mind right beside the look of my father's face on that awful day. Oh God, You are kind to give me this beautiful moment to remember. It helps to ease the pain somehow. He always said we must find something to thank God for in everything that happens. Dear God, I thank you for Grandfather's last smile."

As the morning wore on, the sounds of many people came to her through the thick walls of the ark. There were voices wailing the grief song and others shouting in laughter. Once the angry voice of Koruz could be heard above all others and she crouched lower and covered her head with straw. At the same time there was a scratching on the wall of the bin beside her and the two tigers dropped into the mound in front of her. Her heart almost stopped until she could realize what it was.

They glanced up at the opening of the bin, lashing their tails for some minutes before turning around in the straw and settling. Their bright eyes stared straight at her hiding place for long moments and then with a sigh, they yawned and lay their heads on their paws. Once again their presence comforted her.

"If they are safe here, maybe I will be too," she told herself and tried very hard to believe it.

It was evening before Miriam heard any human steps in the passage below her hiding place. There had been the sound of animals, some with large, ponderous steps, others just scurrying whispers.

"Miriam?" came a quiet voice. It was Loma.

"I'm here."

Loma came up the ladder and dropped down into the bin. The tigers lifted their heads and Loma saw them for the first time. She pushed herself back against the wall beside Miriam.

"Are they really safe?"

"Well, Japheth pets them and scratches their ears. He says they won't hurt anyone unless they are cornered."

"Oh. I hope they know that."

"They make me feel a little safer and not so alone. What is happening at the house? I thought I heard Koruz."

Loma unwrapped some warm cakes and a cluster of grapes and spread them in Miriam's lap. "Yes, he came this afternoon and shouted around about how these people should be out at the river, clearing away the stones. I hadn't seen him close-up before. He is so tall! I can see why people are afraid of him. A lot of the men left after he was there but a few walked with Noah to where Ham and Japheth were digging. The ground is very hard but they will have it ready by tomorrow. Deborah and I have been cooking all afternoon.

"Of course Father took the opportunity to warn them again that God was going to send judgment and that the only way was to repent of their sins and come into the ark.

"They just laughed and hooted and ate some more food before they left. But Koruz left some of his men there so Japheth is afraid to come out. He sent the food and said not to worry. After it is fully dark he will come and stay with you. I slipped out when no one was looking."

"I can't believe that I will not walk with either my father or Grandfather to their graves. That is so wrong. I should be there! It is shameful not to be there. Did my brothers come?"

"Yes, they were here until Koruz came and then they left. Everyone was talking about how they were related to

Grandfather. It seems like everyone is either his descendant or a descendant of his brothers or sisters. It got so boring that I was glad to get away. Even the men who work for Koruz are related someway!"

"Did Uncle Noah tell you how many years he has lived?"

"Yes, at the grave, he showed everyone the time rope and clay tablets on which he had recorded his years. Nine hundred and sixty-nine years. Longer than anyone else. He preached a regular sermon about his name and its meaning. But when he warned them that judgment would now come, they jeered and hooted. Right there beside the grave! It was awful. You can be glad you weren't there."

"But I should have been there." Miriam picked at the meal cakes and tasted a grape. "Loma, do you think the rain will really come in seven days?"

"Well, Ham says he thinks it will. I'm not so sure, but I want to be in the ark, just in case. I think Mother Eva feels the same way but she doesn't want to leave her home. She keeps working but I see her looking around like she can store the room up in her mind and not lose it completely."

"Some things we can never forget. I can't forget the terrible look on Father's face when Koruz struck him. But now in my mind, I can see Grandfather's face. His face seemed to glow when he called his wife's name. Do you think he was really seeing her?"

"I don't know. I'd better be getting back before Koruz's men start asking questions. You know how Father will not lie, so anything can happen. Maybe tomorrow, if not so many come to the wake, I can keep you company in the afternoon. There is lots of wool to spin and that will help pass the time. I think they will have the grave ready by morning."

Back in the house, Noah sat beside the body of his great-grandfather and watched the so-called mourners eat and drink and talk among themselves. The room was crowded and others sat around in the courtyard. The men who worked for Koruz helped themselves to the food lavishly and looked boldly at Deborah and Loma moving quietly among them with the serving trays. There was no sign of grief on any face except those of his own family. His own heart felt so empty and yet in his mind's eye he could see all these people swept away. He had warned them for so many years and they would not listen. His tears came as he thought of the futility of his preaching.

"Not one, Lord. Not one! How can it be that no one will listen any more?" he murmured.

Evalith heard him and came and sat beside him. Her face was drawn with fear as well as grief.

"Will the grave be ready tomorrow?" she asked.

"I think so. It is so unseemly to think that he cannot lie in the cave with his fathers. I can't understand why God has done this."

"Koruz will not tolerate another day of mourning. Those men will be watching to see to that."

"I know. We will move as quickly as we can. Then we'll begin taking the household things into the ark."

"I'm worried for the girls. Those men are staring at them like cats watching a mouse. Should we send them to the ark tonight?"

"No, that might draw the men out there and we can't have that. I want them to come into the ark for safety but they can not come in for evil purposes."

"If they would only stay in the courtyard instead of in here. They make the house seem dirty with all their laughter and stories. They seem to be looking around for something to take. I'm afraid they will break open the wine vat and"

"Perhaps if they drink enough they will sleep and then you and the girls can rest too. The boys and I will sit with Grandfather."

The night wore on and one by one, people slipped away, sated with food and sleepy from the wine. Even Koruz's men nodded and dozed so that finally Deborah, Loma and Evalith retreated to a bedroom and lay down. Japheth sat beside his father and asked, "Should I check on the animals in the ark? They may need water or food."

Noah, remembering Miriam, nodded. "But I may need you here very early. These people will be in an ugly mood in the morning. Did you finish the grave?"

"Yes, it's ready. I will bring spices from the ark when I come in the morning."

"May God guard you through the night."

"And you as well."

Taking care to disturb none of the guests, Japheth eased his way to the front gate and took the path towards the ark. He stopped half way and turned back to see if he was being followed. He stood for several minutes listening and straining his eyes to see the gate. There was a slight sound on the path so he waited motionless, scarcely breathing. He could see no form against the light yet still the whisper of a body moving in the grass neared. Japheth knelt down and held out his hand to check the progress of whatever was there. Suddenly his hand touched a moving form. The long sinuous body of a very large snake glided under his hand, followed by a second one.

"No," he muttered. "Surely we don't have to provide passage for you! You have caused enough trouble in this world. If the flood comes, I hope you all drown."

But they were gone and in the darkness he could not stop them. He could never be sure whether they went up the ramp or around the side.

As he himself reached the top of the ramp, he again stood for many minutes in silence, watching and listening. At last, satisfied that he was not followed, he joined Miriam in what he thought of in his own mind as the tiger's nest. As she ate the fresh cakes that he had brought, he filled her in on the day's news.

"Were my brothers here today? Did they ask about me?"

"Yes, they were here but they left when Koruz ordered all able-bodied men to get back to the river. They said they would come tomorrow for the burial if Koruz would let them."

"They didn't ask if you had seen me?"

"Maybe they asked Father but I didn't hear them."

"If you get a chance, please ask them about my mother and sister. It seems like they are dead too when I don't hear any news of them."

"I will if I can, but it might make them wonder why I'm asking. I'll see if Father thinks it's safe."

"I'm really thirsty. Can I go down now for a drink?"

"I'm sure it's all right now. No one followed me except two very large snakes and I don't know whether they came into the ark or just went around. Come, I'll help you."

Once again in the nest, they settled into each other's arms.

"I'm so afraid. Japheth, do you really think the flood will come this week?"

"Father seems very sure. He seems to be able to hear God as easily as I can tell the needs of the animals. Maybe easier. Anyway, what other choice do we have? If we don't believe him and stay here, we would have to go and throw in our lot with Koruz. Do you want that?"

"Oh no! No, I truly believe there is a God who wants us to obey Him and walk with Him. But Grandfather always said that God loves people. How can He just wash them away?"

"Well, He has given them a hundred years and they have just become more and more wicked. They used to just laugh at Father's preaching. Now it seems to make them angry, at least some of them. They blame him for the earthquake, even though we lost our whole flock that day. Father says that God has said that judgment would come when Grandfather dies. That is the meaning of his name... 'when he dies, it will come.'"

"Loma said you cannot lay Grandfather in the cave because it is gone. Where will you lay him?"

"We have dug a cave into a hillside not far from here. We will lay him there tomorrow. Don't let me forget to take the spices with me in the morning."

"I think I can not bear to sit here another day. I should be there, walking with Grandfather. My own father, and now Grandfather!"

"I will walk in your place, Miriam. We are now one and I will go so a part of you will be there."

Miriam snuggled closer and let the calmness and strength of Japheth quiet her heart. Sleep came at last to both their tired bodies in spite of all that tomorrow might bring.

Chapter Twelve

In the large airy upper deck, Loma and Miriam sat spinning the wool that was piled around them. Sitting on their low stools, their hands were nimble as they twirled the stick on which they were feeding the newly spun yarn. This task needed little thought because through the years their fingers had learned to do it and now they hardly glanced at their work.

"At least we can always make ourselves useful, when we grow old and blind," laughed Loma as they worked.

"I am not planning to be old and blind any time soon," responded Miriam. "Look at Grandfather." He was hundreds of years old and yet he could still see and his mind was still sharp. I hope I have inherited at least a few of his years." She was silent for long minutes as in her mind's eye she was seeing the newly piled stones which marked the grave of her much loved ancestor.

"I still can't believe that I was not able to go with him to the grave yesterday. It seems so wrong! And yet I know the whole family could suffer if I went. It's so hard when everything seems so wrong."

"I know. But you are fortunate to have such a rich heritage," Loma said a little wistfully.

"You haven't told me where you come from, Loma, or how you came to this place. I would really like to hear your story."

Loma sighed. "It is not a very beautiful one, Miriam, and not nearly so exciting as yours. Only God's great mercy is beautiful and it is because of that I am here." She selected a new fleece and expertly joined the fibers to the thread on the spool. "Are you sure you want to hear it?"

"It will help take our mind off these endless days of waiting and wondering what will happen next, that is, if you don't mind telling me. Everyday, I think I just can't stand one more day of waiting."

"I know. It seems almost like we've died already and are just waiting to be buried."

"Oh, Loma. You can think such awful thoughts!"

"I know. But I didn't have a grandfather like yours. Your grandfather used to love to tell of the early days. Instead, that was a subject that was taboo in our house. Oh, it was discussed of course, but never openly and I only learned the story from my mother because I was so curious to know why it was taboo. You see," she paused glancing at Miriam, wondering if she dared to take this risk, "I came from the family of Cain."

Miriam looked up quickly to see if she had heard right.

"From the family of Cain! How? I mean how did you come here if you were from that family. I have never known anyone before from the family of Cain."

"Do you still want to hear about me, now that you know?" asked Loma, her eyes steadily on her work.

Miriam glanced at her. "Yes, I guess I do. More than ever, really," Miriam said a little hesitantly. "Grandfather used to tell me that God was a God of great mercy and kindness, but I didn't know His mercy even included those who were under a... curse. I'm sorry, Loma. I'm being thoughtless but that is what I have always heard."

"Well it is true, Miriam. Our family was cursed with a grandfather who chose to kill his brother. But Father Noah tells me we are all under a curse because of the sin of Adam."

"I never thought of it that way before, Loma." Miriam sat quietly for a few moments deep in thought. Then she continued, "Anyway, I know I'm only here because of God's kindness and mercy so I'd like to hear how He worked to bring you here."

"This is how I learned it," said Loma closing her eyes. Then she began in a singsong voice of one who has recited the words often. "Adam, Cain, Enoch, Irad, Mehujael, Methushael, Lamech, Jubal and Tubal-Cain who had a sister named Naamah. Naamah was my grandmother on my mother's side. She was the youngest in the family and when she grew up, she married one of the sons of Jubal who was her half brother. My mother was born to them very late in their life. They did not ever get around to planning a marriage for her. You see, her hair was curly like mine and she was ridiculed and not considered important. After her parents died, she lived in the house of her brother who worked in the family business of Grandfather, Tubal-Cain.

"You know how he discovered that he could melt iron and bronze out of the stones and then work it into tools and things. Well, all his sons learned the trade and they set up this big oven where they melted the stones. My mother helped the women in the kitchen. It wasn't like your family where you grew up. My great-grandfather Lamech had two wives and many, many children.

"He was a very violent man. He would get angry, just over nothing and many of his sons were like him. People would say, "Oh, he's just hot-tempered like Lamech." If the food was not just what they wanted, they would fly into a rage and throw it at the one who served it. Often they scalded my mother and would beat her and order her to fix them some-

147

thing "fit to eat." She told me about this one time when I was getting older. She was lonely and needed someone to talk to.

"She said that often she hadn't prepared the food, but the wives would always give her the blame. Her life was very hard. Then, as people started to come from far away to buy the tools, my mother found that she could offer herself to them and sometimes for a little while, she felt she was important. They would pay her, of course, and gradually the men of the family realized that this was another source of income. So they set her up in a house near the ovens and while the men waited for their tools to be made, they would send them to my mother.

"I was born in that house many years later when my mother was quite old. I also was the youngest of her many children and had curly black hair, just like hers. I never knew who my father was. He was just one of the many who came.

"When I was little, I could stay close to my mother and life didn't seem too bad because she cared for me. Some of my cousins were musical like Grandfather Jubal and they often came to my mother's house to play for the customers. They had a harp and flutes and of course drums. They played for people while they were eating and earned a bit of gold that way.

"When I got older, I was expected to follow my mother's ways and take up her business but she was hot-tempered too and she loved me and tried to protect me. She said God did not intend for people to live like she did and sometimes I heard her crying and praying that God would deliver me from this wicked life.

"When I was about thirty, still very young you know, my mother died. When that happened, I lost all my protection. Life became almost unbearable. The men who came to buy were sent to me then and I was expected to entertain them. If I refused, which I sometimes did, I was beaten. I wasn't too upset by the beatings because I had seen my mother go through the same thing.

"But then one day, one of the men got the bright idea of trying out the sickle blades on my hair to see if they were sharp enough to satisfy the customers. First they cut just a curl or two and laughed at me when I screamed and shouted at them. One day they cut off all my hair on one side of my head and then made jokes about me because I looked so silly. Of course I wore a head cloth when they would let me, but they loved to jerk it off and tease me. One day, one of the uncles was angry with me for something he thought I'd done. He shaved off all my hair and left me completely bald.

"How could they be so cruel?" gasped Miriam. "I cannot imagine anyone taking such pleasure in cruelty. I hadn't realized how very thankful I should be for my home."

"Didn't your brother's tease and torment you when you were little?"

"Oh yes, of course they did, but never like that. My father wouldn't let them. But these must have been grown men who were treating you that way."

"Yes, they were uncles, cousins and of course my half-brothers. I was not so attractive to men without any hair so I had a little rest for a while as it was growing out. "One of the cousins was particularly cruel. He seemed to take pleasure in hurting things... animals as well as people. He often tried his blades out on the dogs that lay around under the tables. They learned to avoid him, I can tell you. Once when he couldn't find a dog, he decided to try out the knife he was sharpening on my arms."

"See these scars." She drew back the sleeve of her robe. "He made these. I decided then that I would have to run away, but I didn't know where to go. You never know if it will be worse somewhere else. It's hard to find a safe place, and of course no one would plan a marriage for me. I watched the men who came, to see if there was any way I could join myself to some big group of travelers and not be noticed.

"About ten years ago now, Father Noah came to get some new tools. He wanted new axes and sickles. He had traveled a long way and was tired and hungry. They sent him to my house with instructions to feed him and let him sleep there. Of course I expected him to be like all the rest. I prepared food and he thanked me and then to my surprise, he thanked God too. I had never heard anyone do that before. After he ate, he simply went to sleep. I watched him sleep, and thought what a kind face he had. Even though he was tired, he had looked at me but I was afraid to meet his eyes because I knew how men looked at women.

"The next day, his tools were not yet ready, so he ate his meals at my table. He did not like the music and told the boys that they should play to God's glory and not just to make noise and arouse passions. He still had not touched me and was complimentary about the food. During that day he went out and watched the process of making the tools. I could see him talking seriously to the men as they worked. I wondered what he was saying. They didn't seem very pleased with his words and later I learned that he had been telling them of God's coming judgment.

"I heard him tell someone that he came from Uz. Then I knew that he must be from the family of Seth. I had seen many others from that family but none were like Noah. All the others seemed to be just like our family. I wondered what he was like at home with his own people. Was he cruel too? Did he have a temper and was he only being careful because he was far from home and among strangers? I wondered so many things about him but of course I did not ask. Women were not allowed to ask anything. I had learned that lesson painfully because I was a very curious child.

"It seemed peaceful when he was in the house and I began to wish he wouldn't leave. But a few days later one of the uncles came to tell him the tools were about ready and ask him to come and see them. My uncle said I was to come too. My heart suddenly was pounding and I wanted to run. But I was afraid to disobey. I stood back as my uncle laid the axes and sickles on the cloth and they started to bargain the price. Noah picked up the ax and felt the blade to test its sharpness. Then my cousin, who was also standing there, caught me by the arm and dragged me over.

"'I'll show you how sharp it is,' he bragged. He pushed up my sleeve and made a long slice on my arm. He started to do it a second time, but Noah shouted and grabbed his arm. My cousin was so surprised that he dropped the ax and it landed on his foot. He nearly cut off his small toe. He was so angry that he cursed me and he cursed Father Noah. He would have beaten me but he was too busy hopping around holding his toe."

Loma smiled at the memory and then giggled her infectious giggle. "I can laugh about it now, but then I was scared to death because I knew he'd blame me for the accident and there was no telling what he'd do. I really thought he would kill me.

"Father Noah went back to the tools and he and my uncle agreed on a price. I fled back to my house in hopes of delaying the trouble that was sure to come. When his load was ready, Father Noah came to the house and asked to see my arm. I can still remember how I was shaking. He gently pulled back the sleeve and then took some oil from his robe and poured it on the wound. He then tore a strip of cloth from my other sleeve and bound it around my arm. His hands were gentle like my mother's, when I was small. I had never felt any gentleness from any man's hand before. Never! His kindness so touched me that I couldn't help but cry. The tears just flooded over and down my face.

"He stood there quietly for a minute and then he started to talk to God, asking Him to give healing to my arm. He talked to God as if He was right there and he asked Him what he could do for me. He was quiet for a while as though he was listening. You know how he does.

"After a few minutes he sort of nodded and then looked at me. I mean really looked, right into my eyes. I looked down quickly but not before I saw the kindness there in that look. Miriam, you cannot imagine what that look meant to me. I had never seen anyone look like that." Loma paused to wipe the tears from her cheeks.

"Then he said, 'Will you come home with me? My wife needs a good cook to help her with the work. Who is your father, that I may make arrangements?'"

"My mother is dead and I never knew who my father was. My uncle is the one you bought the tools from today. But he will never let me go. Who would do my work, if I went with you?"

"We will see. God has told me to take you with me, so He will make it possible."

"I couldn't say a word. I knew my uncle. He was a cruel, hard man and he got much profit from the men who came to me. He would never let me go unless he got something in return. But I just sat there in my house and remembered that look. He didn't undress me with his eyes like other men did. He looked at me as though I was a much-loved daughter. My mother used to look at me like that sometimes when I was very young. I had never seen that look before in the eyes of any man. A tiny little flame of hope sprang up in my heart. Maybe I could get away. Maybe I would not have to live in that awful place any longer. Maybe God had heard my mother's prayers. It was too much to hope but still I hoped just a little.

"At the same time I was afraid of what was about to happen. You know how it is. You hope for change but at the same time you are afraid it will happen and it scares you because you don't know what the change will mean. At least you are used to the present misery but the unknown is scary.

"I watched through a slit in the window and I could see him talking to my uncle. They seemed to talk a long time and then Father noticed my cousin sitting there with his still-bleeding toe. I saw him go over and speak to him. My cousin tried to spit in his face but he just went ahead and poured oil into the wound and took some cloth from his own sleeve and tied it up. I think my cousin cursed him all the time he was doing this but he didn't pay any attention to his words. Then he went back and pulled down a pack from his donkey and offered my uncle a large bundle of wool. It had been washed and carded and was ready for spinning and it looked very white and beautiful. My uncle could see that it was valuable. Even I could see that it was. But I could see my uncle begin to look at the packs and I knew he was wondering how much more he could get. They talked on for a while and finally Father took down another small bundle and opened it. I couldn't see what it was but I could see by my uncle's face that he was really impressed. Then he put his finger into the pack and quickly put it in his mouth. I guessed then that it was a pot of honey.

"I later learned that in cutting the trees for the ark, he often found swarms of bees and harvested the honey. Since there were few trees in our area, honey was very rare and precious. So Father set the pot down beside the wool and my uncle called me and told me to bring bread and salt.

"They went together to the gate of the city and I took the bread and salt to them. There they dipped salt and ate bread together. Then my uncle took off his sandal and threw it from him. In that way, my uncle gave up his claim to me like I was an old shoe to be thrown away. Father Noah was free to take me as his slave or as his wife or do with me whatever he wanted.

153

"Can you imagine how it felt to me to suddenly be the possession of a kind master? I couldn't believe it at first. How did he persuade my uncle? Why did he let me go? I was so sure that he wouldn't agree. And then I wondered what Noah wanted with me. Did he really want me to help his wife? When he came back to the house and said I was to go with him, I just looked at him like some stupid person.

"Finally he just said, 'Come with me' and he turned around and left. He went out to his string of donkeys and finished putting all his tools and packs back on them. Then he waved his arm for me to come. I was afraid. I wondered if I should go or not. I wondered whether I should take anything with me from that house. I had only one possession that I treasured: a flute that my cousin had given to me and taught me to play. I grabbed that from my room and went out just as I was and got up on the donkey he was holding and we began our journey. No one came to tell me good-bye or wish me well. They just let me go as if I were a cow or a sheep and of no importance to them except as they could use me. That was the big difference. Father Noah looked at me as though I were important to him.

"After a week of traveling, I was exhausted and still scared at what might happen when we got home. On the road, Father Noah had remained so calm and kind, looking after my needs and changing the dressing on my wounded arm. He treated me like his daughter and yet expected me to help with the cooking and packing. I didn't know what to think, and of course I didn't dare to ask anything. I had learned long ago never to ask questions yet I somehow felt that he would answer me and not beat me for asking.

"When we were almost home, we had been walking along the road in silence but my curiosity finally overcame my fear and I said without looking at him, 'Why have you done this?'

"He looked up at me and smiled such a kind smile that I started crying. He said. 'God told me to.'

"'He told me that your mother had cried to Him to deliver you from that wicked life and that He had sent me there to find you.'

"Can God really hear people when they pray?" I asked.

"'Oh, yes. He always hears. He never intended for his people to live like you were living.'"

"That's just what my mother used to say!" I gasped.

"'Well, she was right. God intended us to love each other and to love Him and obey Him. He loves us, you know and He intended for us to be like He is.' He looked so sad as he added, 'but most people do not even try to obey Him any more and they have forgotten how to love Him and each other. They are so eager to learn new things and make new things and make themselves look important. The tree of knowledge is still working in us and we have stopped taking God into account. But God will not let us go on like this much longer.'

"Does God really talk to you?"

"'Oh yes. Every day.'"

"But I don't hear Him."

"'You will, when you are ready to listen.'"

"But I am not like you. I am a daughter of Cain. Everybody always says that God will not hear us because of what he did. And then my grandfather Lamech killed a man too when he was angry over something. So I am sure God will never hear me. I am born under the curse."

"'Yes, that is true,' he answered, 'but so am I.'

I looked at him in astonishment.

"'I am from Adam and Eve just as you are. It is for their sin that we are all under a curse and doubly so because each of us have disobeyed God just as they did.'

155

"I had never thought of that before and my heart sank down even further. What was the use of hoping then? Now I was under a double curse.

"'But God will hear you if you cry to Him from a broken and contrite heart. He is also a God of great mercy and He will not turn you away if you call on Him. I learned this from my grandfather Methuselah who learned it from his father Enoch and also from the lips of Grandfather Adam himself.'

"That was too much for me to take in and I just didn't say any more. The next day we were home. Mother Evalith was very surprised to see me but she made me welcome and put me to work in her kitchen.

"My life was completely changed then. Instead of beatings, I had kindness. Instead of wounds and insults I received gentle words and clean clothes. I learned so many things that I had never known before. I was almost afraid to speak because my language was full of curses and foul words that didn't seem to fit in that house. And that house was often filled with music. Evalith loved to sing and her songs were gentle lilting praises to God. I longed to try to play her songs on my flute but I was still too much afraid.

"I was much needed because Grandfather Lamech was old and weak and required most of Evalith's time to care for him. I watched Deborah and tried to learn how to behave. I couldn't really figure out whether I was a slave or a daughter or what. Father Noah provided everything that I might need but he also expected me to work hard as they all did.

"After a year of living there, I finally plucked up courage one day to ask Evalith if it was true that I could talk to God like they did.

"'Yes, you can call on God if you come to Him humbly asking for His mercy. He will hear you.'

"But what about the judgment that Father Noah keeps talking about. Surely if anyone deserves God's judgment it's me. I haven't loved God nor walked in His ways. I didn't even know what His ways were until I came here. My mother always said we were not supposed to live like we did, but she didn't tell me what God wanted. I don't think that she knew."

"'God's judgment will fall on all who do not repent and turn from their wicked ways. But His mercy is open to all who repent and turn to Him. This is why we make sacrifices to Him. It reminds us that we deserve to die instead of the animal that we are sacrificing and we thank Him for His continued mercy to us.'

"I still didn't understand but I wanted to be like they were, so one night, alone on my bed, I talked to God for the first time. I told Him I wanted His mercy. I told him I was sorry for the mean unkind things I had done and the unloving words I had so often thrown at people around me.

"And He heard me! I know He heard me because suddenly my heart felt like a great stone had been taken out of it. I felt this blanket of warm love wrap around me and it made me so happy I just cried and cried." As Loma spoke the tears overflowed again and both girls were quiet for several minutes. Miriam found her own tears dripping onto her wool and she laid it aside.

"I never knew His mercy was so boundless," Miriam said with wonder in her voice. "I think I have always just taken it for granted. I've asked Him to protect me and I prayed a lot during the week after my father was killed, and when He brought me here, I knew He must have answered my prayer. But then I knew that Grandfather was praying too so maybe it was Grandfather's prayers that brought me here. And I never thought to ask Him for His mercy for all the wrong things I have done. I always wanted to please Him but I haven't always been loving and kind.

"I felt like a warm blanket was wrapped around me that first night in the ark when I was so cold and tired. But then later I realized that it was the tigers that had wrapped themselves around me. It was their warmth I felt."

"But if God sent them to you, wasn't it really His love that warmed you?" asked Loma.

"Oh! I never thought of that!"

"Just like it was God's love that brought Father Noah to me."

Miriam sat turning this over and over in her mind for some time. At last she said, "If God really does love us so much, why is He going to pour out judgment on everyone like Uncle Noah says? I just don't really understand. It doesn't seem to fit together, does it?"

"I know. I thought the same thing. You must ask Father Noah to explain it to you sometime. He says that man's sin is a God-sized problem that requires a God-sized solution and we must trust Him that He really knows what is best. He says more but you should ask him. I can't really understand it, much less explain it."

"But what about my mother and my sister who are living in the house of Koruz? And what about my brothers?"

"I heard your uncle beg your brother to come and join us but he just got up and left the house. He didn't believe what Father Noah said and he wasn't about to stay and listen to any more talk about it."

Miriam sighed. "But doesn't it make you sad to think of your family?"

"Of course it does. Even though they were wicked and cruel to my mother and me, still I don't want to see them destroyed. But Father Noah can help you with that. Talk to him about it."

"Oh look! It's beginning to get dark. I must hurry and help Deborah with the evening meal. The men will be so tired when they get back from the river... or what used to be a river. This wool will still be waiting for us tomorrow."

"I'd better stay here until after dark. Some visitors may still come to sit with the family tonight."

"I'm sure Japheth will come here first when he gets back. If he doesn't, I'll tell him he gets no supper until he does," said Loma with a laugh and disappeared down the ladder.

Miriam smiled too and was just wondering if she should return to her hiding place when she heard heavy steps climbing the ramp. "Japheth," she thought, but it was a rough voice that echoed through the building.

"What have you been doing here?"

"Only spinning wool, sir," came back Loma's rather breathless answer. "If you wish to see Father Noah, he is in the house."

"No, I don't want to see him. Koruz sent me to check this building to see if that girl, Miriam is here."

"There are many animals here sir, and much food for them. But if you are looking for Miriam, you will not find her here. The women at the well think she must be dead. Maybe the tiger killed her."

"Get away woman! What do the women know of these things? Just get out of my way and let me do my own looking."

"The ramp to the lower level is just there," pointed Loma. "Be careful of the wild boar. He can be very fierce."

Miriam listened, hoping the footsteps would go toward the lower ramp but instead they came toward the ladder. Quickly she burrowed in among the fleeces and pulled them hastily over her. In the gathering darkness she prayed that the search would not be too thorough.

Suddenly the animals and birds scattered throughout the ark began a cacophony of sound and far away came the strong rumbling that she had heard the previous week. It came swiftly nearer until the whole ark shuddered and groaned beneath her. She wanted to run but that was impossible. There was a crash and a stream of curses from the man as he fell from the ladder and landed on the large water pot below. The shaking went on for what seemed forever and then subsided. The birds, flying about in panic finally came to rest in the rafters and the donkeys brayed in a kind of a complaint after everything else was still.

Another shaking! thought Miriam. *I hope the men are safe out at the river.* Japheth had told her that his father feared the river would burst out suddenly if there were more shaking. But at least the man Koruz had sent was retreating down the ramp, cursing at every step. She pushed aside a fleece and breathed the dusty air.

"Oh God, thank you for protecting me again. Uncle Noah is right when he says this is a place of safety."

Later, as she lay in Japheth's arms in the bed of straw, he told her of their narrow escape.

"We had just decided it was time to come home because the sun was almost down. We had climbed to the top of the foothill that surrounds what was the valley when the rumbling started and the face of the hill moved and another huge pile of rock came crashing down where everyone had been working. Some were hit by stones and all the work that has been done was undone in a moment of time. We looked to see if any needed help but all were running so we came home. Father says it is the beginning of the judgment. He says that water will both fall from the sky and come up from the deep fountains of the earth."

"It has already been three days since Grandfather died. Do you think the judgment will really come in four more days?"

"The animals seem to think so. Have you seen all the new ones that came in today? There is a pair of young horses, and a pair of camels. The strangest is the elephant pair. They are so fat and their noses reach clear to the ground. Did they make much noise today during the quake?"

"It was amazing to hear them all and they seemed to know it was coming before the noise reached us. Koruz's man was on the ladder and he fell off onto the water pot. His noise was not pleasant. He cursed God and Uncle Noah and everything else he could think of."

"Did he see you?"

"No, I hid under the fleeces but I think he fell before he got all the way up."

"Thank God. Father is quite sure God protects this place. I think we must all move here as quickly as possible. Koruz will be angrier than ever when he gets the reports today. I expect he will find some way to blame Father."

Chapter Thirteen

E valith stood looking at the hearthstone on which she
had cooked meal cakes for all her years as Noah's wife.
How could a thing so old and solidly fixed, skip and move
like a live thing? Horror filled her eyes and tears followed
the furrows in her ashen face. This last movement of the very
earth had lifted this great stone and cracked it in half. How
could that be? She sat down weakly at the familiar table and
automatically began brushing away the fallen debris from
the well-worn top. How could she bear it all? The threats,
the evil, the isolation from family and friends, the death, the
prophesy of destruction, and now her own home falling down
around her. She buried her face in her work-worn hands and
let the silent sobs come. She didn't often weep. It was not her
way, but this was too much. She couldn't bear any more.

Noah, coming in from a quick survey of the damage outside,
found her there, and as he looked around the familiar room
now cluttered with debris, he sighed and sat beside his wife.
Long ago his own hands had set these stone walls in place.
He had cut the beams that made the ceiling. He had laid the
floor stones himself before he ever married. This had been the
home he prepared for his bride and now all these years later, it
lay almost in ruins. The roof tiles had jumped and broken, the

dirt and debris lay everywhere and even the hearthstone was broken in half. He sighed.

"Well Lord God, I can at least thank You for that. I wondered how I would ever get that hearthstone into the ark and now it will be only half the problem. Thank you for that, Lord."

Evalith raised her face and looked at Noah with growing astonishment.

"You can thank God at a time like this!" she shrieked. "Don't you see this house? It is destroyed! It may fall on our very heads as we sleep tonight, if we do, and you thank God for a broken hearthstone!"

"But don't you see, Eva, God is planning for our good. He knows we will not need this house any longer and He is helping us move! Don't you see? This shaking will help us. He knows the difficulties we face.

"But I don't WANT to move from this house. Don't you see! I want to stay HERE. The ark is black and smelly as a tar pit and now filled with so much food and so many animals that I am sure it will never float if the flood does come. And I just don't want to move out of this house."

"Did you feel it!" shouted Loma bursting through the door at that instant. "It really shook! I saw the whole ark jump. Can you imagine? It jumped! And that man from Koruz was in it. He must have fallen because I heard him cursing something awful. And then he came running down the ramp before I got here."

"Do you think he saw Miriam?" Noah asked, distracted for the moment from Evalith's distress.

"No, I don't think so. Shall I go back and see?"

"I think not. You and Deborah should see to your bedrooms. They will need some work before you can use them tonight."

As Loma went off to find Deborah, Noah moved closer and put his arms around Evalith's shaking shoulders and drew her tightly against his chest. It seemed so clear to him. Why couldn't Evalith see it as simply as he did? God had said the time was now. What could be simpler? But he wisely kept these thoughts to himself and only prayed aloud.

"Lord God Almighty, Maker of heaven and earth, You made us and we are Yours. I pray that You will fill Evalith's heart with Your peace tonight. Look down in mercy, Lord and comfort her heart with Your presence. Make her know deep down that our only safe place is with You and wherever You lead. Help us, Lord! We are beset on every hand. You see the enemy who wishes to destroy us and the ark that You have commanded. Give us Your protection tonight, Lord. We look only to You. Protect the ark tonight and all that is within. Bless Shem and Deborah, Ham and Loma, Japheth and his new bride. Keep us safe for Your own Name's sake for our trust is in You."

Little by little, as he prayed, a quietness filled the room and Evalith's body stopped trembling. At last she drew a long sigh.

"How can He do that?" she whispered at last. "When He draws near, He seems to breath peace back into me. Thank you Lord God for drawing my heart back to you. Without You we would be just like all the others in this city."

She rested against Noah for a moment more and then vigorously scrubbing her face with her sleeve, she got up and moved toward the bedroom.

"Let's see if we have a bed to sleep in. I haven't had the courage to look in there yet."

Noah followed her, his sandals crunching on the gritty sand covered floor. The lamp threw a sad glow over the sleeping platform now covered with dirt from the ceiling. Evalith quickly brought the broom and began brushing the room and platform clean. Then taking the folded blankets outside, she shook them vigorously and brought them back and began the familiar task of preparing the bed for sleep: first the heavy quilt filled with straw, then the soft goat skins that comforted their skin. Finally she spread the woolen coverlet that had served them for so many of their years together. When it was ready, she took the broom and began sweeping the main room. Deborah and Loma, their faces a study in contrasts, came from their rooms. Deborah was pale, her face set in rather grim lines of determination. Loma looked excited and chattered busily as her hands flew about the supper tasks.

"I thought it must be a great herd of cattle coming our way or elephants or something. Then when the shaking started I thought the house would come right down on top of you. The trees just whipped back and forth like mad things. Do you think it will come again, Deborah? I hope it doesn't. I don't like it when the earth shakes. But then I do like it a little bit. It is so exciting! Don't you think it is exciting Deborah?"

"No, I don't," Deborah, replied shortly. "Look at the hearthstone! It's broken in two!" They stood and stared until Evalith broke the silence.

"Just build the fire. We must get some food ready at once."

While they were busy with this, Noah gave his attention to the precious box that contained the family records. It had been loosened from the niche in the stone wall but was not damaged. He looked inside and breathed a prayer of thanks that the tablets were still there and not broken by the earthquake. He carried the heavy chest to the dining table and set it down with a sigh. He must take it to the ark at once. These records must be preserved. How could he have waited so long?

The evening meal was eaten quickly and Japheth, with Miriam's portion concealed in his cloak, went out into the dark front garden and watched a long time before proceeding to the ark. Shem and Ham were tired and soon retired to their respective rooms with their wives.

Evalith took a last hungry look around the room, feeling some comfort that it was at least neat and tidy if not thoroughly clean. At last she moved to the bedroom and stretched her tired body on the bed. Noah followed, laid aside his outer robe and lay beside his wife. She nestled close for comfort, her cheeks once again wet with tears but Noah had extinguished the light and did not see them.

In silence Evalith lifted her heart to God once more. "Lord God, You see my heart. How can I leave this familiar place? This is my home. Here my sons were born. Here in this room I have lived with this man these long years in peace and sorrow, in youth and now in old age. How can I go out from this place? My roots grow deep here like the great trees that grow in the yard. You will have to help me tomorrow. I cannot do this without Your help.

"For Deborah and Loma it will not be so hard. Perhaps they will enjoy the change and at least Loma will see it as an adventure. Deborah will see it as a task that must be done and done well. But for me, it feels like the very end of life. Can a tree be transplanted when it is old? Will the roots take hold anywhere else? Will there ever BE anywhere else?"

A gentle snore from Noah indicated that he was already fast asleep.

How can he sleep when this will be our last night in this house? she thought. *It may even be our last night on earth.*

Her heart that had been filled with peace a short time ago erupted in a storm of worry. She had heard the rumors, the murmured confidences that Deborah and Loma shared over the beating of the flax. She knew there was talk in the market of burning the ark and this house and all of them. This house was made of stone and would provide some safety but the ark was covered with pitch, both inside and out. It would burn like a torch. How could she bear to go into it? And Noah slept on so calmly! As this whirling circle of worry and fear drew ever tighter and tighter around her, she finally cried out to God in desperation.

"Lord God, You see my fears and all our lives are in Your hands. Help me to trust You. Help me to stay in that peaceful place near You. Draw near again Lord God. I need You."

Evalith drew closer to the reassuring back of her sleeping husband and little by little the tightness in her chest began to ease and because the day had been long and active, sleep did come at last.

When morning light began to creep into the bedroom, Evalith woke with a start and dressed quickly. Noah was already up, as was his custom. Remembering the events of the night before, she quickly went out to assure herself that all was in order. Deborah was already pounding the grain and Loma was preparing to start the fire.

She gathered up the wool that was beside the table, waiting for idle moments of spinning. Taking it to the door, she shook it carefully and tucked it into a wool bag outside the door. Then taking the reed broom, she began to sweep the room. Each stone of the floor, worn into familiar patterns seemed precious. Many were concave from endless passing steps.

Noah came through the door as she was finishing.

"No need to clean it so carefully, Eva. We will carry everything into the ark today."

"Well, I will not leave it dirty! What would people think that came in here after we are gone?"

"No one will be here to see it and God will wash it cleaner than you can."

Evalith continued her careful sweeping saying silent good byes to each stone.

"Are we really moving today?" asked Loma from beside the hearth where she was tending the meal cakes.

"Yes, God said it is time. He will open the windows of heaven and pour down a cleansing rain to wash this dirty world. He also says He will break open the fountains of the great deep and we must be safely aboard the ark before that happens."

Loma's eyes sparkled with excitement.

"I like the ark, except for the smell. It feels so safe there. But how will we cook? Surely we can't have a fire there."

"When you finish this morning, we will carry the hearth stones to the ark and make a place where a small fire can be built. But we will have to use great care and keep it in an earthen pot."

"We can put the coals in this earthen pot when we finish," put in Deborah. "I'll make sure it doesn't go out or get spilled."

"What about this table?" asked Evalith, running her hand tenderly over its scarred surface. "Can we take it with us?"

"Why not? The boys will be happy to carry it for you."

She unhooked the loom from the large carved hook on the wall and wound the long warp threads carefully around the wooden frame that kept them separate. Then taking the strap that passed around the weaver's back to provide the perfect tension, she wrapped it around the bundle and rolled the whole thing in a piece of woven cloth that was still in process. Tucking the shuttle in securely, she laid them outside the door beside the bundle of wool. As she did so, she glanced toward the ark and was astonished to see a steady stream of animals moving up the ramp. There were two delicate deer, gingerly testing the ramp and sniffing the air with obvious distaste.

Smiling a little grimly, she thought, *I feel the same way about that smell, little ones. But we will get used to it.*

In spite of herself she felt the pull to run to the ark and join that parade. Yet another force warred within, urging her to run back into her safe familiar stone house and hide.

169

"Oh Lord God, help me be obedient like those dumb beasts. They seem to obey without question. Why can't I?"

Japheth was standing in the doorway at the top of the ramp, grinning like a small child. She beckoned him to come but he just waved and continued to watch. He would rather watch animals than eat. Not so Ham, who came down the ramp quickly, dodging animals and nearly getting tripped by the big lizard that was scrambling up. Shem followed him down and they came to the gate grinning.

"Did you ever see such a sight, Mother? We're going to be knee deep in animals soon. There will be no place to stand," said Ham.

"Come and eat now. Father wants everything loaded today. You can take some to Japheth and Miriam after you have eaten."

As the family gathered around the low table to eat, Noah suddenly looked at Loma.

"Loma, do you have any record of your family that we can carry into the ark today?"

"No sir. Only me. I'm the only record I have that I ever had any family but yours."

"But we should preserve your history, otherwise, how will anyone ever know? You uncle surely had such a record."

"Oh yes. He had one, but he seemed like he didn't want to remember. But my mother taught me the names when I was small. I can say it for you and teach it to my children, if God ever blesses me with children." She made a wry face that was meant to be funny but instead revealed deep pain. She collected herself quickly and continued, "But I don't have any ages like you do. No one kept count of our years."

"This morning you must recite it for me and I will write it on clay tablets. Then you must carry it into the ark and store it safely there. It is important to remember who you are. I do not know why I waited so long."

So it was that while the rest worked all day, carrying and storing, Loma sat with Noah and waited as he recorded each name back to Adam.

The shadows were long before the task was finished. They had been so intent that they did not see Koruz until he was standing at the gate with his small cadre of men.

"Why is it that you refuse to help your townsmen? I saw none of you at the river today," he shouted.

"Koruz! You surprised me. Please excuse me for not greeting you properly. My hands are wet with the clay from these tablets. We were just preserving the family records. It is my task as oldest in my family since Methuselah has gone. Surely you understand that this is a week of mourning for us."

"We cannot allow the luxury of mourning. I have come to warn you personally that I expect all your sons at the river tomorrow. If they are not there, I will send my men to persuade you."

"It'll make a great sight," put in one of the men. "I expect it will light up the whole city if we wait till it gets dark and bring our torches."

"I also have a warning for you, Koruz. I know you do not honor the Creator God but still I must tell you that tomorrow God will send rain and floods upon the earth. The only place of safety will be in that ark. There is room for all who wish to escape. God has been patient through all this century, waiting and giving you time to repent. God is a God of mercy. He does not rejoice in the death of the wicked. Repent and come instead into the place of safety with us. Otherwise you will die."

Koruz threw back his head and laughed loudly and his men jeered and began pushing at the gate, some gathering stones and heaving them over the fence at Noah. Loma quickly backed into the house, but Noah sat still, shielding the still wet tablets from the falling stones.

"Send them away Lord God. You are our hiding place," Noah said softly.

"He thinks his God can protect him," Koruz shouted to his men. "Tomorrow we will show him who is God in this place. Tomorrow there will be only ashes left to scatter in the wind. We will see then what you are hiding in that ark. I'm wondering whether you have seen that blond niece of yours that was promised to me some weeks ago. If you are hiding her, it will go hard with all of you."

"Wherever she is, she is in God's hands, Koruz."

Koruz stood for a moment staring hard at Noah's back and then with a shrug he turned and he and his men moved back down the street shouting curses and threats as well as ribald comments as to their intentions for the morrow.

Noah sat sadly shaking his head. "If they only knew You, Lord. But they choose not to know You. Surely tomorrow the very heavens will weep over all these people who would not come to You. I feel an echo of your pain, Lord and burn with anger at their contempt for You. I am not worthy of Your loving care, but I do love You and want to serve You. I pray that my sons will be faithful to You as well, honoring You and obeying You in everything. Lord if even one generation fails to pass along Your truth, all the succeeding generations will not know who You are. Oh God, preserve a remnant in each generation to carry Your love to the next. Otherwise we will become ravening beasts as these have become who think they are so wise."

Evalith came from the house, her face pale in the fading light.

"I heard them, Noah. They really intend to burn the ark."

"Yes, if they could, they would. But God is still God. He is able to protect us."

"The hearth stones are still here. Shall we eat here and then in the morning the stones will be cool enough to carry."

Noah listened quietly a moment and then nodded briefly. He had two more names to add and then he would be finished.

As the family gathered around the table that night the house around them was empty except for the few cooking utensils needed for their supper and their bedding. Japheth joined in the meal, fearful lest his absence would be noted by any who were watching.

Questions swirled in all their minds but it was only the talkative Loma that expressed them.

"How long do you think it will be before we eat in a house again? Will we come back to this house after the flood? Do you think the rain will come from the sky like from a waterfall, all in one place, or will it be scattered around?"

"Loma, wait a minute," Ham interrupted with a laugh. "How can anyone begin to answer your questions when you ask another one without taking a breath? Let Father have a moment to at least nod or shake his head."

Noah cleared his throat and looked lovingly at Loma.

"It's all right, child. I, too, have many unanswered questions and to those that you just asked I have to say I don't know. We have never gone this way before. We are starting a journey that has never been done, so naturally there are many uncertainties. Our only certainty is in God and the fact that He loves us. We have followed His instructions down to the very last daub of pitch and we can only hope that we will again see our dear house and fields again."

"But what if you are wrong? What if Koruz does burn down the ark and everything in it dies? What then? Does that mean that there isn't any God or that He is not so powerful as you think?" This from thoughtful Shem.

"God has never answered my 'what if' questions. He just says, 'Trust me and all will be well.' The only 'what if' question He has spoken about is the 'What if we don't obey Him.' He has made it clear, then, that we will surely perish."

At that moment there was a rasping sound from outside and the stone wall that had been loosened by the shaking of the earth trembled enough to bring more sand and gravel down through the cracked ceiling.

"Earthquake!" exclaimed Loma, jumping up.

"No, I don't think it's that," said Japheth. It may be another guest for the ark. Just a minute. I'll see."

In the deepening twilight Japheth made his way toward the continuing sound. As his eyes became accustomed to the darkness, he saw the round bulbous form of the river horse intent on scratching his itchy skin on the corner of the house.

"You should make life interesting in the ark, my friend. We may have to find a scratching pole just for you so you don't break anything."

Sticking his head back inside the house for a moment he said loudly for the benefit of any outside listeners, "It's just a river horse. I'll walk the pair of them to the ark and see that they are bedded down."

In the darkness, he did not see the one who stood in the deep shadows at the foot of the ramp watching his slow progress towards the ark.

In the large corner room that Shem and Deborah had shared all their years together, Deborah was folding their day garments and quickly spreading the goatskins that made their sleeping comfortable. As she stretched her long stately form beside Shem, the conversation at the table was still whirling around her mind.

"Shem, do you really think there will be a flood tomorrow? What if it doesn't happen? What will we all do then? It doesn't seem that there is any future for us either way."

"I know, Deborah. If the flood comes, will we survive to plant and harvest again? And if it doesn't come, will we survive to plant and harvest again? It is just one of those times when everything seems to be ending."

"It frightens me, Shem." Deborah moved closer and Shem slid his arm around her and drew her close. "Loma seems to be enjoying it, but I just have this big knot of fear inside that won't go away."

"We just have to trust in God. What else can we do? If we don't trust God enough to obey Him, then we must obey Koruz! Surely we don't want to do that. He is an evil man. He kills for pleasure. He pretends to be helping the people with his water project, but really he is just growing rich at their expense. Everything he does is for his own personal purpose. And if he wasn't strong enough to get people to obey him, then others would rule and do the very same thing. No one looks to anyone's needs and wants but their own. And they hate Father because he is not like them."

"Why do they hate him so much? He hasn't done anything to any of them except try to save their lives."

"I know, but you remember hearing the stories of Cain and how angry he was at Abel. The same spirit is at work in everyone who does not believe in God."

"Do you think they will burn the ark?"

"I'm not sure. We'll just have to trust the Lord God. I have talked to Father about trying to strike back or defend ourselves but he wisely pointed out that we are only one family and even our own close relatives are not with us. We must simply trust God and obey Him. Where else can we go?"

"But it seems like there should be something we could do. Is there no one we can appeal to? When I look at the future it looks as black as that ark."

175

"Deborah, go to sleep. Tomorrow we will carry our bedding into that black ark. Remember that you mustn't build the fire on the hearth in the morning. We want the stone cool enough to carry."

"What will we do for breakfast?"

"We'll eat something cold, perhaps. Just go to sleep."

"I must get the coals into the fire pot. I must do it now while the coals are still alive."

"We will see to it in the morning."

But Deborah was already up, moving like a shadow into the main room where the fire still cast a faint light. She quickly shoveled the coals into the fire pot and dropped in a few hard knots of wood to keep it alive till morning. Then using the shovel, she spread the remains of the fire so it would die. As she sat watching the coals lose their glow and fade into the blackness, she felt a part of herself was dying too. She had tended this hearth fire all the thirty years of her marriage to Shem. It had been her province to see that it did not go out. Now she was deliberately letting it die. All the sadness and uncertainty of these last days seemed to gather into a great ball of pain and lodge in her throat. If only she could cry, perhaps it would be a relief. Dropping one last knurl of wood into the pot, she gratefully crept back to her bed and drew close to the back of her sleeping husband. She must simply accept these things that she could not change. Father Noah often said that in acceptance, there was peace. She hoped he was right.

Chapter Fourteen

Noah opened his eyes in the gray pre-dawn and looked at his still sleeping Evalith. *Let her sleep a few more minutes.. It will be a difficult day and she will need all her strength to get through it.* Then the truth of what day it was struck him and propelled him out of bed.

"Eva! Today is the day! We must go quickly to the ark. This is the day we have been preparing for all these long years."

Evalith woke with a start and quickly began dressing and folding up the bedding. She would not think about it. She would just do it. There would be plenty of time to think later.

In the kitchen, Noah was calling to the family and making sure that all were awake and busy.

"But what about breakfast?" asked Ham. "Surely we have time to eat before we begin."

"Here are some of the cakes that were left last night. I saved them for you," Loma responded. "You can eat them on the way to the ark. Here. Take them and some figs. We can eat when we get everything moved."

It was a strange procession that soon was making its way across the harvested fields to the great black mouth of the ark. Evalith, carrying their bedding, felt she was walking toward her tomb. Shem and Ham were struggling with half of the hearthstone, Ham with a meal cake clenched in his teeth. Deborah had the pot of hot coals balanced on a heavy towel on her head and both Noah and Loma had their precious boxes of clay tablets. As they neared the ark, Japheth came down the ramp to meet them and Miriam stood watching from the doorway.

As Japheth stepped off the ramp, Koruz's man emerged from beneath it. Glancing up toward the doorway, he caught sight of Miriam just as she turned away.

"So! You have been hiding her! I knew we'd find her if we waited long enough. Bring her out so I can take her to Koruz at once."

"She is my wife, you fool! Koruz has no right to take her from me. Go back and tell him that she is already married."

"He cares nothing for that. I'll collect a large reward for finding her and he'll give you no rest until she is safely in his harem."

Shem and Ham had reached the ramp by this time and as they slowly made their way past Japheth there was no way Koruz's man could get up the ramp. Noah edged past the two and proceeded up the steep walkway as though nothing were happening. Evalith, Deborah and Loma followed him.

Koruz's man, seeing that he was outnumbered, turned toward town.

"I'll be back. We'll turn that ark upside-down and shake you all out. If that doesn't work, we'll set it on fire. That will bring you all out in a hurry."

With a string of curses he started down the road toward town.

The three women looked at each other and continued on up into the ark.

"He will be back!" whispered Miriam as Noah moved down the passageway beyond her.

"Yes, no doubt he will be back and bring a great hoard of people with him. We will simply have to trust the Lord." He carefully fitted the box into a niche he had long ago prepared for it. "Here Loma, give me your box. They will both fit here together."

"But Koruz will kill all of you now that he knows I'm here. Japheth, we must run away, far away, before he gets back! If we stay here, it will only bring death to all of you. Come Japheth!" She grabbed his arm. "Let's run. We can be far away before they realize that we have gone."

Noah, hearing her words, came back and put a hand on her trembling shoulder.

"Miriam, God has brought us to this place. It is the only place of safety. If you run away, you will only perish in the flood. Come. Climb up into the upper deck and help Evalith get things arranged.

"Boys, leave the stone here in the passage and go back and get the rest of it. Japheth and I will get the table and the rest of the bedding."

Miriam stared at him wide-eyed for a long moment. Should she run down the ramp and give herself to Koruz? She could run and hide again as she did that long, awful week. But the words of Grandfather seemed to echo through her mind.

"Go to Noah!"

Having obeyed then, it seemed foolish to go out now. Japheth took her hand and led her to the ladder.

"Go up and help Mother. God has not done all this to let us die at the hand of Koruz. Look around you. See the animals. God has sent them here. We must trust Him just as they do."

Reluctantly she climbed the ladder and instead of dropping into the bin of straw, she went on to the large airy upper deck.

"Here Miriam. You can watch the fire pot while Loma and Deborah run back and get the rest of the bedding. We must get things arranged so they can eat and drink when they come back."

"Shouldn't I hide somewhere, perhaps in the straw bin where I was before?"

"I think the hiding time is past, Miriam. If God does not help us now, none of us will survive. We must simply trust Him." Her voice was grim as she spoke but her actions were resolute as she began sorting out the food from the stores all around her.

"I'm not so brave as you, Mother Eva. I just want to run."

"I know. I want to run too. But God is watching. He knows. And no matter how we feel, we must still do what we know is right."

"Here, put one more knot into the fire so it won't go out."

Mechanically, Miriam obeyed while her mind raced toward a dozen possibilities at once. Soon the family was back, clambering up the ramp. Shem and Ham quickly began tying the stone to the rope they had used for the hay. With much effort and many starts and stops they at last had the great hearthstones up to the third level where they slid them onto the platform filled with sand that Noah had built for them.

As Loma and Deborah came up the ladder, Loma shouted.

"Here they come! The men from the market are coming! Father and Japheth are just about here with the table."

"Leave the table and come in," shouted Evalith. "We don't need the table."

But Noah and Japheth continued with the heavy table until, with a sigh, they set it down just inside the passageway.

Noah turned and saw a great crowd of men, many with sticks and weapons in their hands, shouting and each one trying to get ahead of the other. Their curses fell harshly into the quiet of the ark.

Then, within the ark, a great symphony of animal sound erupted: birds flew wildly, the elephants trumpeted and from below came the doleful howl of the wolves. They looked at one another questioningly and then in the distance the now familiar rumbling rolled toward them. The ark began to creak and shake under their feet and suddenly, the great heavy door which was firmly propped open above the ramp came down with a crash. The props flew far down the passageway and the door that was itself covered with pitch, closed with a thump. Pitch oozed out around the edges sealing it securely.

The women, drawn by the noise and confusion stared down at the great blackness that had been an open door just a moment before. The shaking continued for what seemed like an age and then abruptly stopped. In the dimness the family looked at one another, speechless with amazement. At last Noah found his voice.

"God has shut the door! He has shut the door! I could never have done it. Maybe just one of them wanted safety instead of to harm us. But God, Himself, has shut the door!"

Noah bowed his great shaggy head into his pitch-stained hands and wept.

Little by little the animals quieted themselves until there was a great stillness throughout the whole length and breadth of the ark. Outside could be heard, more faintly now, the curses of the men and the shouts of the crowd. Occasionally someone pounded on the now closed door and demanded Miriam be brought out. But finally the great bellowing voice of Koruz came through clearly.

"Send out the girl or we will set the place on fire!"

When only silence answered him, he cursed and pounded at the door, but finally gave up and ordered his men to go and get tools so that the door could be opened.

Inside the women huddled together taking comfort in each other. Below Noah began to pray.

"Lord God, Maker of heaven and earth, we have done as You commanded. Hear their threats and protect us. We are in Your hand. Our trust is in You. Look down in mercy and spare us from the wrath of men."

Once again the earth trembled as if in answer to Noah's prayer. The noise outside the ark subsided and in the dim light the animals and birds settled themselves.

"Can they open the door?" asked Loma shakily.

"Look! The beams we had prepared to hold it closed have fallen into place during the shaking. No, Loma," answered Ham, "there is no way that they can open that door now. We might as well go and have our breakfast."

"But what about Koruz? He'll bring them back and they will set fire to the ark. Then what will we do? We can't open the door to get out!"

"Never mind, Miriam. Can't you see that the door was shut by God's hand? That closed door is good news. It means our God is truly in control," Japheth answered, climbing quickly up to where she stood with the other women. "You are truly safe now," he said as he reached the upper level and drew her to him.

"But I don't feel safe."

"I know. We can't trust our feelings. I think not one of us feels safe. But we are in God's hand and we are doing God's will. That is the only safe place there is in this world."

"Come and have some food. We haven't broken our fast yet this morning," Evalith called to the men who were still below.

"Here Shem. You and Ham get the table up to the next level. I will check the door to make sure it is well sealed and then I will join you," said Noah.

As the family gathered around the familiar table, its surface marked by centuries of use, Evalith caressed it lovingly.

"It makes me feel just a little at home to have our table here."

"I feel the same way about the hearth stones." said Deborah. "I have used them so many years that they seem like old friends even if they are broken."

"I feel I should be helping Grandfather begin his day," murmured Miriam wistfully.

The tigers that had been prowling around restlessly since the last earth temblor came and lay down beside the table and looked expectantly at Japheth.

"They like figs," he said fondly and took some from the table for them.

"What can we do now, Father? Just wait for them to come back and set the place on fire?" Shem asked a little sharply.

"My son, what else can we do? They hate us without cause. They want Miriam for evil purposes. Their only desires are to do wrong. They are very like our Uncle Cain who killed his brother because of envy and jealousy. Our own hearts are much like them and if we started to defend ourselves, where would it end? God has said, 'Vengeance is mine. I will repay.' We must allow Him room for that."

"But will He repay? That is the question, isn't it?" put in Ham, "and will He repay before we are all dead?"

There was a murmur of assent around the table.

Noah sighed deeply. "That is His business, isn't it? He does not answer to us but we to Him. Yet I cannot believe that He would cause me to build this great ark of safety and send all these animals to us, if He did not intend to save us. Look around you. The animals that have come here are content and most of them curled up asleep. Let's borrow from their faith. Even a little faith is better than none."

There seemed to be no answer to that and after taking a bit of food and drink, they sat listening for sounds of renewed attack from the outside.

"It seems so strange to be finished. We have hurried and worked so hard for so long that I can not just sit down and do nothing," said Ham. "Come on Japheth. Let's look around and see who all we have in here."

"I think our work is not done," Japheth answered with an uneasy smile. "We still have to feed all these creatures and see whether Father's system for cleaning the stalls is going to work. We will have plenty to do. Come on Shem, we can use all the help we can get."

As the three men moved off to see to their new charges, Noah sat still at the table, looking at Evalith. Deborah and Loma cleared the table and Miriam checked the small fire pot and carefully fed it a piece of wood. Evalith's face was white and set as she ran her fingers over the rough table. From outside came the sounds of the returning town's people and the smell of burning torches crept into the ark through the opening that ran all around under the roof. The women stopped, frozen in silence, listening to the great voice of Koruz demanding that Miriam come out. Miriam looked at Noah but he only gave his head a brief shake. She sat trembling on the hearth and Deborah squatted beside her, putting an arm around her shoulder.

As the moments passed, the room seemed to darken. From far away came the rumble such as they had not heard before. A dark pall seemed to be falling over the ark and the people outside grew quiet. In this stillness a new sound like the rush of many tiny feet on the roof above was heard. The room continued to darken and then there was a brilliant flash of light and a deafening clap of thunder. The women screamed and huddled together, trying to shut out the world around them. The noise on the roof grew to a mighty rushing sound.

"Look!" shouted Noah, "It's raining! See it dripping from the edges of the roof! It's raining!"

Another flash and roar of thunder brought the three men clambering up the ladder.

"What's happening?"

"Is it fire? Have they set fire to the ark?"

"No, look!" shouted Loma, "It's raining! See it running off the roof!"

"Why is it so dark?" Shem asked. "It's like evening already."

The noise of the rain grew to a rushing roar making talk impossible. Outside the ark, Koruz and his crowd dropped their torches in the quickly forming mud and ran for the city. Just as Noah had prophesied, the windows of heaven were open and the rain was coming down. Then with a great shudder, the earth moved under them and that face of the mountain, from which the quiet stream had so recently flowed, burst outward and all the pent up water roared forth. Far away, the earth was torn open and the fountains of the great deep burst out. Water gushed up from below and poured down from above.

The hours passed with only the sound of the roaring rain. The family clung to each other and cried to God for His mercy. The ark began to lurch and creak, the beams so carefully cut and fitted together bearing the great strain of weight until finally the great wall of water from the springs of the mountain bore it up on top of the waves. It floated free.

Noah gazed around him in awe and then lurching to his feet on the unsteady floor, he looked at Shem.

"It floats! Just as God planned, it floats. All this weight, all the food, all these animals, even the tons of pitch we put on it, it still floats! Praise God!

"Come, we must sing the song of praise that is from the before time. Never must we let it die. God must be praised in all the earth."

So above the roar of the rain, in the one dry place in all the earth, Noah and his family lifted their shaky voices in praise to the God who had rescued them from all their enemies and made a safe place for them in the midst of His judgment.

Epilogue

I
t was a steep climb but Miriam savored the rain washed air as she helped two-year-old Gomer up the steps. His head was covered with golden ringlets and his blue eyes reflected the deep blue of the sky. How sweet the air! How beautiful the sky with the billowing clouds against the deep blue! After the long dark year inside the ark, she would never again take such sights and smells for granted.

"Bow, Mother! See the bow!" Gomer said excitedly as he reached the top step and could see the graceful arch of color.

"Yes, Gomer, I see the rainbow. Wasn't God kind to give us such a pretty bow?"

"Here, Gomer," called Grandmother Evalith from her seat by the wall. Come and tell me the colors."

"Blue!" Gomer answered excitedly, pointing to the sky.

"Yes, the sky is blue but what color is the bow?"

"Bow pretty!" he answered as he climbed into her lap.

They were gathered on the rooftop of the sturdy stone house that Noah and his sons had built after they came down the mountain from the ark. After living so long with the pitch covered walls, the white stones, the green growing trees and vines were a rich feast for their eyes. Tents had been their home at first and even now they dotted the fields, giving shelter from the hot noonday sun. Each day seemed better than the last. Noah gazed fondly as the rest of the family gathered around him on the roof.

Shem and Deborah were the last to arrive, Deborah cradling the newest arrival, Arpachshad in her arms. Ham and Loma's two sons, Cush and Mizraim, pushed close to gently touch the tiny sleeping face. Noah sighed as he looked at them all.

"God is good!" he said at last. "He has given us a new beginning. Evalith, just look at those grandchildren and another soon to come."

"Four lovely boys and more to come. I hope we will have some granddaughters as well. God must know that these boys will need wives."

"Of course He knows. He always plans for our good. He will not forget such an important thing as that. Remember how He planned wives for our sons, even in the midst of that wicked world when there was no one left who believed."

"I remember. But I am afraid too. I guess I have been afraid so long that I don't know how to expect good instead of evil."

"What could you possibly be afraid of now, Mother," Japheth asked. "All the wickedness has been washed away. The world is new. We are free to build it in God's way. There is no one left to fear."

"But still I fear. I am afraid we will forget. I'm afraid we will grow careless or cruel or proud. If we fail to teach even one of these children about our God and all that He has done then his children will not know and their children will not know. I'm sorry. I didn't mean to spoil such a lovely evening. Forget the worries of an old woman."

Noah reached out and took her tiny hand in his great one. "Your fears are warranted. God Himself has told me that we must be careful to teach His ways to all our children. We still carry in our bodies the seeds of sin and we must fear lest we grow careless and forget God."

"But so many of the things we feared never happened." Loma said. "We were afraid we would never have children. Yet, look at them. God was kind in keeping us from bearing children before the flood. I felt so angry when you said that before the flood, Father Noah, but now I know that they might not have survived in that dark cave for so long. Now they can run and play in the sunshine and grow strong and healthy."

As though this were an order, both boys began to caper around the roof and Loma stationed herself across the opening to the stairway to contain their exuberance.

"The thing that makes me sad," Japheth said, "is that the animals no longer trust us. Have you noticed? They fear us. Even after all those long months in the ark when we fed and cared for them, now they have changed."

"God has done that, Japheth. Remember that He said He would put the dread of us on every animal. Perhaps it is necessary for their survival or so they won't be dependent on us. But they are prospering too. Have you seen the new crop of lambs and goats? Our herds have doubled in these two years, in spite of the sacrifices we have made. And now that I do not have to spend every day building, I can give myself to the growing plants. This is a great joy to me. I love the land and to see the vines and trees growing, to watch the grain that lay all year in the ark, now spring up to produce more grain... this is surely a little of the way it was in the beginning, before the curse."

"Father, did you ever doubt that God would send the flood?" asked Ham, gently peeling his two-year-old off his back and handing him a bit of cane to chew.

"I doubted myself often. I doubted that I would get the ark built properly or that it would float. God spoke so clearly about the flood that I could not mistake that. But I wondered often if the ark would float."

"I wondered if it would ever stop floating," laughed Loma. "I'm so glad to be on dry ground again. My stomach never liked all that movement."

Quietness settled over them as the sun disappeared behind the young olive trees. At last Noah began the ancient hymn of praise and even the children tried to join in.

"Think of it my children," Noah said at last, "in all the world, we who are here in this place represent all that God has planned for this world. Has He not blessed us more than we deserve? And yet, even in these blessings there is danger that we will forget His great mercy and become proud and selfish and unloving."

"How could we ever forget how He shut the door and sent the rain," asked Shem. "We all owe Him our very life. These children would never have been born but for His mercy. He had mercy even when my faith was so small."

"I will never forget that day when I looked up into my husband's eyes and he quickly covered me with his load of straw," Miriam said. "I began to feel protected that day."

"I will never forget that God has delivered me from the curse of my father's house and given me a new home," Loma whispered.

"I am glad God has taken away my reproach and given me this child." said Deborah, touching her sleeping son's face tenderly. "In him there is hope for the future and comfort from the past."

"Indeed it is true." said Noah. "My sons, I charge you to guard these memories and events well and teach them carefully to all your children that none may ever forget all that we owe to God our Creator. Teach them to love Him and walk in His ways. Then all will be well in every generation."

And God drew near and wrapped them in His cloak of night and smiled.

"I know the plans that I have for you," He whispered. "Plans for good and not for evil—to give you a future and a hope."

About the Author

Aflair for the dramatic, a deep understanding of God's love for people and a strong feeling that I had an important message for this generation were my motivations for writing this book.

Academically, I had one year at Northwestern Bible College and forty years of experience as a missionary and mother of four. Living and working within the Asian culture with its binding relationships and intense friendships has taught me in ways that academic degrees could not do.

I grew up on a farm in Iowa, the youngest of a warm Christian family. As a teen, I gave myself unreservedly to the Lord. I married a man who was also called by God and after he completed his studies, (I got my PHT degree—putting hubby through) we joined Far East Broadcasting Co. and have worked in Asia ever since. We first went to Manila, Philippines but later were assigned in many different places. In Singapore, I filled in as an English teacher at the Singapore Bible College for one year. I sure learned more than the students! I taught English as a second language both in Singapore and later in Okinawa. In Okinawa I developed my own material for teaching English to 4 and 6 year olds. I taught Bible studies in the cross-cultural setting most of the time but during one home assignment, I wrote and presented a

Bible study for the women of Whittier Area Community Church, in California. The group averaged around 100 each week. I have also done some speaking at women's retreats.

During our last ten years in Manila, I counseled cross-culturally, answering all the letters that were addressed to Dr. Harold Sala's daily radio program, Guidelines for Living. I also handled some of the more urgent letters addressed to the Insight For Living program of Chuck Swindoll. These letters were from our listeners in the Philippines and I learned much about the Asian family structure and found Biblical ways of helping them in their complex interpersonal relationships. I worked under a fully trained Filipina counselor. This on-the-job training was most useful in knowing how Asians think and behave within their families. For this reason, my book has a distinctly Eastern flavor.

Printed in the United States
93075LV00007B/91-120/A

9 781600 340666